HIGHLAND FLING

Sally and Walter Monteath rashly agree to act as host and hostess at a shooting party at Dalloch Castle, in the wilds of Scotland. Joined by their friends Jane Dacre and Albert Gates they do their level best to entertain an interesting, if not bizarre, assortment of house guests. Disaster curtails the sojourn, but already their lives and circumstances have changed forever. Broke before this adventure even started, Sally and Walter can expect to suffer even more financial problems before long—whilst Jane must persuade her parents to accept and welcome the somewhat affected and artistic Albert Gates into the family.

HIGHLAND FLING

NANCY MITFORD

A New Portway Large Print Book

CHIVERS PRESS
BATH

First published 1931
by
Thornton Butterworth
This Large Print edition published by
Chivers Press
by arrangement with
Hamish Hamilton Ltd
and in the USA with
Sterling Lord Literistic Inc.
at the request of
The London & Home Counties Branch
of
The Library Association
1992

ISBN 0 7451 7323 3

British Library Cataloguing in Publication Data available

To
HAMISH

CHAPTER ONE

Albert Gates came down from Oxford feeling that his life was behind him. The past alone was certain, the future strange and obscure in a way that it had never been until that very moment of stepping from the train at Paddington. All his movements until then had been mapped out unalterably in periods of term and holiday; there was never for him the question 'What next?'—never a moment's indecision as to how such a month or such a week would be spent. The death of his mother during his last year at Oxford, while it left him without any definite home ties, had made very little difference to the tenor of his life, which had continued as before to consist of terms and holidays.

But now he stood upon the station platform faced—not with a day or two of uncertain plans, but with all his future before him a complete blank. He felt it to be an extraordinary situation and enjoyed the feeling. 'I do not even know,' he thought, 'where I shall direct that taxicab.' This was an affectation, as he had no serious intention of telling the taxi to go anywhere else than the Ritz, as indeed a moment later he did.

On the way he pretended to himself that he was trying hard to concentrate on his future, but in fact he was, for the present, so much enjoying the sensation of being a sort of mental waif and stray, that he gave himself up entirely to that enjoyment. He knew that there would never be any danger for him of settling down to a life of idleness: the fear of being bored would soon drive him, as it had done so

1

often in the past, to some sort of activity.

Meanwhile, the Ritz.

An hour later, he was sitting in that spiritual home of Oxonian youth, drinking a solitary cocktail and meditating on his own very considerable but diverse talents, when his best friend, Walter Monteath, came in through the swing doors with a girl called Sally Dalloch.

'Albert, darling!' cried Walter, seeing him at once, 'easily the nicest person we could have met at this moment.'

'How d'you do, Sally?' said Albert getting up. 'What's the matter, why are you so much out of breath?'

'Well, as a matter of fact it's rather exciting, and we came here to find somebody we could tell about it; we've been getting engaged in a taxi.'

'Is that why Walter's face is covered with red paint?'

'Oh, darling, look! Oh, the shame of it—large red mouths all over your face. Thank goodness it was Albert we met, that's all!' cried Sally, rubbing his face with her handkerchief. 'Here, lick that. There, it's mostly off now; only a nice healthy flush left. No, you can't kiss me in the Ritz, it's always so full of my bankrupt relations. Well, you see, Albert, why we're so pleased at finding you here, we had to tell somebody or burst. We told the taximan, really because he was getting rather tired of driving round and *round* and *round* Berkeley Square, poor sweet, and he was divine to us, and luckily, there were blinds—which so few taxis have these days, do they?—with little bobbles on them and he's coming to our wedding. But you're the first *proper* person.'

2

'Well,' said Albert, as soon as he could get a word in, 'I really do congratulate you—I think it's quite perfect. But I can't say that it comes as an overwhelming surprise to me.'

'Well, it did to me,' said Walter; 'I've never been so surprised about anything in my life. I'd no idea women—nice ones, you know—ever proposed to men, unless for some very good reason—like Queen Victoria.'

'But I had—an excellent reason,' said Sally, quite unabashed. 'I wanted to be married to you frightfully badly. I call that a good reason, don't you, Albert?'

'It's *a* reason,' said Albert, rather acidly. He disapproved of the engagement, although he had realized for some time that it was inevitable. 'And have you two young things got any money to support each other with?' he went on.

'No,' said Walter, 'that's really the trouble: we haven't; but we think that nowadays, when everyone's so poor, it doesn't matter particularly. And, anyway, it's cheaper to feed two than one, and it's always cheaper in the end to be happy because then one's never ill or cross or bored, and look at the money being bored runs away with alone, don't you agree? Sally thinks her family might stump up five hundred a year, and I've got about that, too; then we should be able to make something out of our wedding presents. Besides, why shouldn't I do some work? If you come to think of it, lots of people do. I might bring out a book of poems in handwriting with corrections like Ralph's. What are your plans, Albert?'

'My dear . . . vague. I have yet to decide whether I wish to be a great abstract painter, a great

3

imaginative writer, or a great psycho-analyst. When I have quite made up my mind I shall go abroad. I find it impossible to work in this country; the weather, the people and the horses militate equally against any mental effort. Meanwhile I am waiting for some internal cataclysm to direct my energies into their proper channel, whatever it is. I try not to torture myself with doubts and questions. A sidecar for you, Walter—Sally? Three sidecars, please, waiter.'

'Dear Albert, you are almost too brilliant. I wish I could help you to decide.'

'No, Walter; it must come from within. What are you both doing this evening?'

'Oh, good! Now, he's going to ask us out, which is lovely, isn't it? Sally darling, because leaving Oxford this morning somehow ran away with all my cash. So I'll tell you what, Albert, you angel, we'll just hop over to Cartier's to get Sally a ring (so lucky the one shop in London where I've an account), and then we'll come back here to dinner at about nine. Is that all right? I feel like dining here tonight and I think we'll spend our honeymoon here too, darling, instead of trailing round rural England. We certainly can't afford the Continent; besides, it's always so uncomfortable abroad except in people's houses. Drink your sidecar, ducky, and come along.'

'Cartier will certainly be shut,' thought Albert, looking at their retreating figures; 'but I suppose they'll be able to kiss each other in the taxicab again.'

At half-past nine they reappeared as breathlessly as they had left, Sally wiping fresh marks of lipstick off Walter's face and displaying upon her left hand a large emerald ring. Albert, who had eaten nothing since one o'clock, was hungry and rather cross; he felt exhausted by so much vitality and secretly annoyed that Walter, whom he regarded as the most brilliant of his friends, should be about to ruin his career by entering upon the state of matrimony. He thought that he could already perceive the signs of a disintegrating intellect as they sat at dinner discussing where they should go afterwards. Every nightclub in London was suggested, only to be turned down with:

'Not there *again*—I couldn't bear it!'

By the time they had finished their coffee Sally said that it was too early yet to go on anywhere, and that she, personally, was tired out and wanted to go home. So, to Albert's relief, they departed once more, in a taxi.

The next morning Albert left for Paris. It had come to him during the night that he wished to be a great abstract painter.

CHAPTER TWO

Two years and two weeks later Albert Gates stood on a cross-Channel steamer, watching with some depression the cliffs of Dover, which looked more than ever, he thought, like Turner's picture of them. The day was calm but mildly wet, it having, of course, begun to rain on that corner of a foreign field which is forever England—the Calais railway station. Albert, having a susceptible stomach, was thankful for the calm while resentful of the rain, which seemed a little unnecessary in July. He stood

5

alone and quite still, unlike the other passengers, most of whom were running to and fro collecting their various possessions, asking where they could change money and congratulating each other on the excellence of the crossing. Every mirror was besieged by women powdering their noses, an action which apparently never fails to put fresh courage and energy into females of the human species. A few scattered little groups of French people had already assumed the lonely and defiant aspect of foreigners in a strange land. Paris seemed a great distance away.

Albert remembered how once, as a child, returning from some holiday abroad, he had begun at this juncture to cry very bitterly. He remembered vividly the feelings of black rage which surged up in him when his mother, realizing in a dim way that those tears were not wholly to be accounted for by seasickness, tiredness, or even the near approach of another term at school, began to recite a dreary poem whose opening lines were:

> 'Breathes there a man with soul so dead
> Who never to himself hath said,
> "This is my own, my native land? . . ."'

She did not realize that there are people, and Albert among them, to whom their native land is less of a home than almost any other.

He thought of the journey from Calais to Paris. That, to him, was the real home-coming. Paris, the centre of art, literature and all culture! The two years that he had just spent there were the happiest of his whole life, and now the prospect of revisiting England, even for a short time, filled him with a

6

sort of nervous misery. Before the two years Albert had never known real contentment. Eton and Oxford had meant for him a continual warfare against authority, which to one of his highly-strung temperament was enervating in the extreme.

He had certainly some consolation in the shape of several devoted friends; but, although he was not consciously aware of it, these very friendships made too great a demand upon his nervous energy.

What he needed at that stage of his development was regular, hard and congenial work, and this he had found in Paris.

So happy had he been there that it is doubtful whether he would ever have exchanged, even for a few days, the only place where he had known complete well-being for a city which had always seemed to him cold and unsympathetic, but for two circumstances. One was that Walter and Sally had written even more persuasively than usual to beg that he would stay with them in their London flat. He had not seen them since that evening when they dined with him at the Ritz, and Walter was the one person whom he had genuinely missed and found irreplaceable.

The other circumstance—the one that really decided him—was that he had recently shown his pictures to a London art dealer of his acquaintance, who had immediately offered to give him an exhibition the following autumn. As this was a man of some influence in the London world of art, owning the particularly pleasant Chelsea Galleries where the exhibition would be held, Albert felt that here was an opportunity not to be missed. He arranged therefore to bring over his pictures immediately, intending to store them and look

7

about for a studio where he himself could stay until the exhibition should be over, late in October. Paris was becoming hot and stuffy and he felt that a change of air would do him good. Also, he was really very much excited at the prospect of seeing Walter again.

Presently the ship approached the quay, and sailors began adjusting a gangway at the very spot where Albert stood. Inconsequently he remembered the landing of the Normans—how William the Conqueror, springing first from the boat, seized in his hands a sod of English soil. It would be hard to do that nowadays. Impossible even to be the first to land, he thought, as he was brushed from the gangway by a woman of determined features laden with hand luggage which she used as a weapon.

In the train he found himself sharing a carriage with two idiotic girls who were coming home from a term at some finishing school in Paris. They were rather obviously showing off on his account. After talking at some length of their clandestine affairs with two French officers, which appeared to consist solely in passing notes to them when visiting the Louvre on Thursday afternoons, but which they evidently regarded as the height of eroticism, they broached the subject of Art. It appeared that once a week they had spent two hours at some *atelier* drawing the death mask of Beethoven, the Venus of Milo and other better known casts in smudgy charcoal. These depressing efforts were now produced from a portfolio and pinned on to the opposite seat which was unoccupied. Albert learnt from their chatter that when a drawing was finished by a pupil at the *atelier*, 'Madame' would come round and add *'Quelques petits accents bien à leur*

8

place'; in other words, the finishing touch. The pupil would then fix it and put it carefully away in the portfolio.

Presently one of the girls said:

'I think I must go on with my art, I might make quite a lot of money. You know, Julia once made two pounds by painting lampshades for her mother's dining-room, and I'm quite as good as she is.'

The other one remarked that she thought Art was marvellous.

They then began to play vulgar jazz tunes on a portable gramophone, a noise which Albert found more supportable than their chatter.

As the train drew near London he felt homesick and wretched. He longed to be back in his studio in Paris surrounded by his own pictures. It was a curious and rather squalid little abode, but he had been happy there and had grown attached to it. His neighbours had all been poor and friendly, and in spite of having seen practically none of his English friends and few French people of his own class for two years, he had not for a moment felt lonely.

Now he began to wish that he had never left it; the pouring rain outside the carriage and the young artists opposite him had plunged him into a state of the deepest gloom. The idea of seeing Walter again began to terrify him. Walter! How could one tell what changes a year of matrimony may not have wrought. Considering these things, Albert fell asleep in his corner.

When the train stopped at Victoria he got out drowsily, but was only half-awake until suddenly thrown into a most refreshing rage by the confiscation, from his registered luggage, of a copy of *Ulysses* which Walter had particularly asked him to procure.

'Sir!' he cried violently to the uninterested official, 'I am Albert Gates, an artist and seriously-minded person. I regard that work as literature of the highest order, not as pornography, and am bringing it to London for the enlightened perusal of my friend Monteath, one of your most notable, if unrecognized poets. Does this unutterable country, then, deny its citizens, not only the bodily comforts of decent food and cheap drink, but also the consolations of intellect?'

At this point, observing that his audience consisted of everybody on the platform except the one individual to whom he addressed himself, he followed his porter to a taxi and was soon on his way to Walter's flat in Fitzroy Square.

Driving up Grosvenor Place he was struck, as people so often are when returning from an absence abroad, by the fundamental conservatism of London. Everything looked exactly the same as it had looked the very day that he left, two years before. The streets were wet and shiny, as they had been then; the rain fell in the same heart-rending drizzle, as though it had never for a moment stopped doing so, and never would again. The same Rolls-Royces contained hard-faced fashionable women in apparently the identical printed chiffon dresses and picture-hats of two years before, fashionable, but never *chic*.

He though how typical it is of Englishwomen that they should always elect to dress in printed materials. A passion for fussy detail without any feeling for line or shape.

'And those picture-hats which have been worn

10

year after year, ever since the time of Gainsborough and which inevitably destroy all smartness, they seem still to be blossoming upon all heads, in this repulsive town. If ever I marry, God send it may be a woman of taste.'

Albert disliked women, his views on the sex coinciding with those of Weininger—he regarded them as stupid and unprincipled; but certain ones that he had met in Paris made up for this by a sort of worldly wisdom which amused him, and a talent for clothes, food and *maquillage* which commanded his real and ungrudging admiration.

These and other reflections continued to occupy his mind, until, looking out of the window, he saw that the taxi had already arrived in Charlotte Street. He was now seized with the miserable feeling of nervousness which always assails certain people when they are about to arrive at a strange house, even though it should belong to a dear friend of whose welcome they are inwardly assured. He began to torture himself with doubts. Suppose Walter had not received the telegram announcing the day of his arrival, and they were spending a week-end in the country? Or, worse than that—for he could easily go to an hotel if it were necessary—suppose they had really not wanted him at all, or had put off some visit on his account, or—but at this moment the taxi stopped abruptly opposite a green front door which was almost immediately opened by Walter. At the sight of his friend's welcoming face, Albert's doubts vanished completely.

'My dear!' cried Walter, 'my dear boy, my darling Albert. *How* we have been looking forward to this! Oh, how nice to see you again after all these

11

years! Quickly! quickly—a cocktail. You must be dying for one. And here's Sally, who's been spending the whole day arranging flowers in your bedroom.'

'I do hope you won't die of discomfort here,' said Sally. 'Did Walter prepare you in the least bit for what you're going to suffer? There are no servants, my dear, except an idiot boy. You know, the sort that murders butlers in the evening papers, but he's quite sweet really, and as we haven't a butler we think it's fairly safe. Cocktail for you?'

The room into which Walter and Sally led the way was so lovely that Albert, who had half expected the usual green horror with sham 18th century flower pictures, was thrown into a state of almost exaggerated rapture. For a London drawing-room it was a particularly good shape, with large windows and cheerful outlook. The walls were covered with silver tissue a little tarnished; the curtains and chair covers were of white satin, which the grime of London was rapidly turning a lovely pearl colour; the floor and ceiling were painted a dull pink. Two huge vases of white wax flowers stood one each side of the fireplace; over the mantelpiece hung a Victorian mirror, framed in large white shells and red plush. Albert, as he walked about the exquisite room, praising and admiring, felt blissfully happy; the depression which had been gathering force ever since he left his studio that morning now left him for good.

He had always experienced in Walter's company a feeling of absolute ease and lack of strain. He now found, rather to his surprise, that the presence of Sally did nothing to impair their relationship; she gave him no sensation either of intruding or of

12

being intruded upon. Walter and Sally together seemed almost like one person, and Albert realized at once how wrong he had been to oppose their union.

'How I should like,' he said, looking at her lovely face, 'to paint a portrait of Sally.'

'Well, why not? She'd love to sit for you, I know, and we've got a room with a perfectly good north light at the back of the house. Albert, *do*.'

'My dear, impossible. I can't work in London, you know. People think it an affectation, but I assure you that it is no such thing. I might even go so far as to say that I'm incapable of working in this country at all; a question, I suppose, of nerves.'

'How like Walter,' said Sally laughing. 'Poor angel, he's quite incapable of working in London, too. He gave up his last job after exactly three days.'

'Shut up, darling. You know quite well who it was that begged and implored me to leave, now don't you? Sally's father,' explained Walter, 'got me a job in a bank. I can't tell you what I suffered for three whole days. It was like a P. G. Wodehouse novel, only not funny at all, or perhaps I've no sense of humour. To begin with, I had to get up at eight every morning. One had much better be dead, you know. Then, my dear, the expense! I can't tell you what it cost me in taxis alone, not to mention the suit I had to buy—a most lugubrious black affair. There was no time to get back here for luncheon, and I couldn't go all day without seeing Sally, so we went to a restaurant which was recommended to us called "Simkins," too putting off. Sally was given some perfectly raw meat with blood instead of gravy, and naturally she nearly

13

fainted, and she had to have brandy before I could get her out of the place. By then we were so upset that we felt we must go to the Ritz in order to be soothed, which meant more taxis. In the end we reckoned that those three days had cost me every penny of thirty pounds, so I gave it up. I can't afford that sort of thing, you know.'

'Poor father,' said Sally, 'he's very much worried about Walter. He has a sort of notion in his head that every man ought to have some regular work to do, preferably soldiering. He doesn't seem to understand about cultivating leisure at all, and he regards writing poetry as a most doubtful, if not immoral occupation.'

'And he isn't as bad as your uncle Craigdalloch, who actually said in my hearing of some young man, "Ah, yes, he failed for the Army, and was chucked out of the City, so they sent him to the Slade." Just think how pleased Tonks must have been to have him!'

Walter then asked Albert how long he intended to stay.

'Can you keep me till the end of next week?'

'My dear, don't be so childish. Now that we have at last persuaded you to come, you must stay quite a month if you won't be bored. I know London in August is very unfashionable, but it would cheer us up a lot to have you, and besides, think what a boon you would be to the gossip writers!'

'Yes, indeed,' said Sally, 'poor old Peter seems to be at the end of his tether already. His page the last few days has been full of nothing but scraps of general knowledge which one assimilates quite unconsciously. I call it cheating . . . I mean, when I want to read about wild ducks sitting on their eggs

14

at the edge of a railway line I can buy a book of natural history; but I do like gossip to *be* gossip, don't you? This paragraph about the ducks was headed, "Observed by Jasper Spengal." Well, I was quite excited; you know what a talent Jasper has for observing things he's not meant to, and then it was only the beastly old duck after all. Well, I *mean* . . . If he's come down to that sort of thing already, it will be the habits of earthworms by August, I should think.'

'So you want me to stay and have my habits noted instead?' Albert felt all his resolution slipping away. After all, it was nice to see his old friends again. It occurred to him now that he had been very lonely in Paris.

'But you'll be leaving London yourselves?'

'Not until the end of August, anyhow, then we may go to the Lido for a little.'

Walter looked rather defiantly, like a naughty child, at Sally as he said this, and she pretended not to hear. She knew quite well, and had said so already more than once, that, terribly in debt as they were, this idea of going to the Lido was quite out of the question. Sally spent much of her life trying to put a brake on Walter's wild extravagances and they had more than once been on the verge of a quarrel over the Lido question.

The Monteaths led a precarious existence. They had married in the face of much opposition from both their families, especially Sally's, who looked upon Walter as a rather disreputable, if attractive, person and an undersirable son-in-law. However, as soon as they realized that Sally was quite determined to marry him whatever happened, they had softened to the extent of settling five hundred

15

pounds a year on her. More they could not afford. Walter had about the same, which had been left him some years previously by an uncle; they struggled along as best they could on a joint income of one thousand a year. This they supplemented from time to time by writing articles for the weekly papers and by the very occasional sale of one of Walter's rather less obscure poems.

All might have been well except for his incurable extravagance. In many ways they were extremely economical. Unlike the type of young married couple who think it essential to have a house in the vicinity of Belgrave Square and a footman, they preferred to live in a tiny flat with no servants except an old woman and a boy, both of whom came in daily. Sally did most of the cooking and all the marketing herself and rather enjoyed it.

On the other hand, Walter seemed to have a talent for making money disappear. Whenever he was on the point of committing an extravagance of any kind he would excuse himself by explaining: 'Well, you see, darling, it's so much cheaper in the end.' It was his slogan. Sally soon learnt, to her surprise and dismay, that 'it's cheaper in the end' to go to the most expensive tailor, travel first class, stay at the best hotels, and to take taxis everywhere. When asked why it was cheaper, Walter would say airily: 'Oh, good for our credit, you know!' or 'So much better for one's clothes,' or, sulkily: 'Well, it is, that's all, everybody knows it is.'

He also insisted that Sally should be perfectly turned out, and would never hear of her economizing on her dresses. The result was that during one year of married life they had spent exactly double their income, and Sally had been obliged to sell nearly all her jewellery in order to pay even a few of the bills that were pouring in, so that the idea of going to the Lido, or indeed doing anything but stay quietly in London was, as she pointed out, quite ridiculous.

Walter, incapable always of seeing that lack of money would be a sufficient reason for giving up something that might amuse him, was inclined to be sulky about this; but Sally was not particularly worried. She generally had her own way in the end.

CHAPTER THREE

After dinner that evening, Walter said that Albert's first night in England must be celebrated otherwise than by going tamely to bed. Albert, remembering with an inward groan that Walter had always possessed an absolutely incurable taste for sitting up until daylight, submitted, tired though he was, with a good grace; and at half-past eleven they left the house in a taxi. Sally was looking particularly exquisite in a dress which quite obviously came from Patou.

Walter, explaining that it was too early as yet to go to a night-club, directed the taxicab to the Savoy, where they spent a fairly cheerful hour trying to make themselves heard through a din of jazz, and taking it in turns to dance with Sally.

After this, they went to a night-club called 'The Witch,' Walter explaining on the way that it had become more amusing since Captain Bruiser had taken it over.

'All the night-clubs now,' he told Albert, 'are run

by ex-officers; in fact it is rather noticeable that the lower the night-club the higher is the field rank, as a rule, of its proprietor.'

Presently they arrived in a dark and smelly mews. Skirting two overflowing dustbins they opened a sort of stable-door, went down a good many stairs in pitch darkness and finally found themselves in a place exactly like a station waiting-room. Bare tables, each with its bouquet of dying flowers held together by wire, were ranged round the walls, the room was quite empty except for a young man playing tunes out of Cochran's revue on an upright piano. Albert was horrified to see that Walter paid three pounds for the privilege of merely passing through the door into this exhilarating spot.

A weary waiter asked what they would order. A little fruit drink? Apparently no wine of any sort could be forthcoming, not even disguised in a ginger-beer bottle. They asked for some coffee but when it came it was too nasty to drink. This cost another pound. Depression began to settle upon the party, but they sat there for some time valiantly pretending to enjoy themselves.

'Let's go on soon,' said Walter, at the end of an hour, during which no other human being had entered the station waiting-room. They groped their way up the stairs and bumped into a body coming down, which proved to be that of Captain Bruiser. He asked them, in a cheerful, military voice, if they had had a good time. They replied that they had had of all times the best, and thanked him profusely for their delightful evening. He said he was sorry it had been so empty, and told them the names of all the celebrities who were there the night before.

After this, they sat for some while in a taxi, trying to decide where they should go next. The taximan was most helpful, vetoed 'The Electric Torch' on account of having as he said, 'taken some very ordinary gentlemen there earlier in the evening,' and finally suggested 'The Hay Wain.' 'Major Spratt is running it now, and I hear it is very much improved.'

To 'The Hay Wain' they went. Albert felt battered with fatigue and longed for his bed. This time they approached their destination by means of a fire-escape, and when they had successfully negotiated its filthy rungs, they found themselves in a long, low, rather beautiful attic. There were rushes on the floor, pewter and wild flowers (which being dead, slightly resembled bunches of hay) on the tables, and the seats were old-fashioned oak pews, narrow, upright, and desperately uncomfortable.

A waiter, dressed in a smock which only made him look more like a waiter than ever, handed them a menu written out in Gothic lettering. Ten or twelve other people were scattered about the room, none of them were in evening dress. They all looked dirty and bored.

'Is Rory Jones singing to-night?' asked Sally.

'Yes, madam; Mr Jones will be here in a few moments.'

An hour and a half later Rory Jones did appear, but he had just come from a private party, was tired, and not a little tipsy. After singing his best known and least amusing songs for a few minutes, he staggered away, to the unrestrained fury of Major Spratt, who could be heard expressing himself outside the door in terms of military abuse.

19

'Let's go on, soon.'

'On,' thought Albert wearily, 'never bed?'

The next place they visited, run by a certain Colonel Bumper, was called 'The Tally-Ho' and was an enormous basement room quite full of people, noise and tobacco smoke. It appeared that champagne was obtainable here, owing to the fact that the club had been raided by the police the week before and was shortly closing down for good.

Albert thought of Paris night-clubs with some regret. He felt that 'The Hay Wain' and 'The Witch' might be sufficiently depressing, but that 'The Tally-Ho' induced a positively suicidal mood—it had just that atmosphere of surface hilarity which is calculated to destroy pleasure.

'Let's go on soon,' said Walter, when they had drunk some very nasty champagne. Despite the cabman's warning, they now went to 'The Electric Torch' but found on arrival that the 'very ordinary people' had gone. Moreover the band had gone, the waiters had gone. Alone, amid piled up chairs and tables placed upside down on each other, stood the proprietor Captain Dumps. He was crying quite quietly into a large pocket handkerchief, and never saw them come or heard them creep silently away.

After this, to Albert's ill-concealed relief, they went home. It was half-past five and broad daylight poured in at his bedroom window. He calculated with his last waking thoughts that this ecstatic evening must have cost Walter, who had insisted on paying for everything, at least twenty pounds, and he felt vaguely sorry for Sally.

CHAPTER FOUR

The following afternoon at about half-past three Sally and Walter got out of bed and roamed, rather miserably, in their pyjamas.

The daily woman had come and gone, and Albert's room proved, on inspection, to be empty. After a lengthy discussion as to whether they could bring themselves to eat anything and if so, what, they made two large cups of strong black coffee, which they drank standing and in silence. Sally then announced that she felt as if she were just recovering from a long and serious illness and began to open her morning letters. 'Bills, bills, and bills! Darling, why did we hire that Daimler to go down to Oxford? There must have been trains, if you come to think of it.'

'Yes, but—don't you remember?—we hadn't an A.B.C. We couldn't look them up. Give the bill to me.' He took it from her and began to burn holes in it with his cigarette, but Sally, engrossed in a letter, did not notice.

'Who's that from?'

'Aunt Madge. Listen to it:

'MY DEAREST SALLY,

'"You will no doubt have seen in the newspapers that your Uncle Craig has been appointed chairman of the mission to New South Rhodesia . . ."

'Of course I haven't! Does she imagine that I have nothing better to do than read the papers?'

'Go on,' said Walter.
'Where am I? Oh, yes!

'"... This was all very sudden and unexpected and has caused us inconvenience in a thousand ways, but the most unfortunate part of it is that we had arranged, as usual, several large shooting parties at Dalloch Castle. I wrote and asked your father and mother if they would go up there and act as host and hostess, but Sylvia tells me that they have to pay their annual visit to Baden just then. It occurred to me that perhaps you and Walter are doing nothing during August and September, in which case, it would be a real kindness to us if you would stay at Dalloch and look after our guests. I know that this is a big thing to ask you to do and, of course, you must say no if you feel it would be too much for you. If you decide to go we will send you up in the car and you must invite some of your own friends. Dalloch will hold any amount of people.
'Yrs. affecly.,
"MADGE CRAIGDALLOCH.

"PS.—General Murgatroyd, a great friend of your Uncle Craig's, will be there to look after the keepers, etc."'

There was a long silence. Walter sat down rather heavily.
'Well?' said Sally.
'Well, what?'
'Shall we do it? Listen, my precious. I know it would be awful and I expect you'd simply hate it, poor sweet, and nothing to what I should, but still,
22

facts must be faced. If we do this we shall save money for two solid months, and after that, if you like, we could probably afford to spend a little time in Paris, if we could let the flat. Albert might be able to tell us of some nice cheap hotel there.'

Walter became sulkier every minute.

'I won't stay at a cheap hotel in Paris. Paris to me means the Ritz. I'm very sorry—it's the way I'm made. Besides, it's well known to be cheaper in the end to stay at the Ritz, because otherwise one has to keep taking taxis there to see who's arrived. And I won't let the flat. It never pays to let houses, because of all the damage that is done by tenants.'

'Perhaps we could manage to have a week at the Ritz if we went to Scotland, funny creature,' she said, tickling the back of his neck.

Walter laughed and began kissing her hand, one finger at a time.

'What d'you think, then?'

'How d'you mean? What do I think?'

'Walter, you're being extremely tiresome, darling. You know quite well what I mean.'

'My precious angel, I've often noticed how clever you are at getting your own way, and if you've really made up your mind that we've got to have two months of potted hell in Scotland I suppose nothing can save us. But I should just like to say here and now, that I'm quite sure it would be cheaper in the end to go to the Lido. I know you wouldn't think so but these economies always lead to trouble; I've seen it so often.'

'But, darling, we haven't even to pay our railway journey if we go in the car, and there can't be any expenses up there.'

'Well, mark my words. Anyhow, if we go, let's

23

make Albert come too, and then we might get some fun out of it.'

'Yes, of course, and we could ask some other chums. Jane, perhaps. It won't be too bad really, you know. Sweet darling, not to make a fuss—are you sure you don't mind terribly? Shall I ring up Aunt Madge now?' She kissed the top of Walter's head and went over to the telephone.

'Hullo? Is Lady Craigdalloch there? ... Mrs. Monteath ... Don't wander about, Walter, it puts me off. No, don't—that's my coffee ... Hullo, Aunt Madge? Sally speaking ... Yes, we've just got it ... Well, we think we'd love to ... No, sweet of you. Can we come and see you sometime and talk it over? ... yes, of course, you must be frightfully. When do you go? ... Oh, goodness what a rush for you! ... Yes, we could be there in about half an hour ... All right, we'll meet you there ... No, perfect for us. Goodbye!'

Sally hung up the receiver.

'Where d'you think we've got to meet them? You'd never guess, but it's so typical of them, really. The House of Lords! So come on, my angel, and dress, because I said we'd be there in half an hour.'

＊   ＊   ＊

Sally and Walter were perched rather uncomfortably on a red leather fireguard in the Prince's Chamber of the House of Lords. The magnificent personage, of whom they had inquired whether they could see Lord Craigdalloch, presently returned from his quest for that nobleman. 'His lordship says he may be a little

24

time, but I will inform her ladyship that you are here. Meanwhile, would you wait a few moments?' He walked rather pompously to the other end of the room where he stood motionless.

'Well, he doesn't seem to be informing her,' said Sally, 'unless by telepathy. Still, I'm quite happy here, aren't you? Of course, it just *is* one's spiritual home, that's all. *Why* didn't I marry a peer? I'd really forgotten what a divine place it is, such ages since I've been here.'

'Like church, isn't it? I keep expecting the organ to peal forth. It rather reminds me of our wedding in some ways.'

'More like a mausoleum, really. D'you see that very old man over there?'

'I see the seven oldest living creatures, if you mean one of them.'

'The one with the greenish face over by the statue of Queen Victoria.'

'My dear, I hadn't noticed him. But how awful! Can't we help in some way? Is he dying?'

'Oh, I expect sort of vaguely he is. This place mummifies people you know, without their having to die first, and they often go on creeping about like that for years. That's why they're called Die Hards. It is a most descriptive name for them, poor old sweets. Anyway, that particular one is a great friend of daddy's, and he disinherited his eldest son for marrying a Catholic.'

'Not really? It's rather heavenly to think such people do still exist. What happened to the son, though—was he quite broke?'

'Oh, no, not at all; the Catholic was immensely rich. So, to pay the old boy out, they took the grouse moor next to his in Scotland and started a

25

stoat and weasel farm on it and quite soon all his grouse were eaten up by weasels. Daddy says he never got over it—it nearly broke his heart.'

Walter looked round him for a few minutes in silence. 'I haven't seen anybody the least aristocratic-looking yet,' he remarked presently, 'except, of course, the boy friend who is by way of informing your aunt that we are here. He's a lovely man, but all the others look exactly like very old and decrepit doctors. I can imagine any of them pulling out a thermometer and saying, "Well, well, and how are we to-day? Put out your tongue and say 'Ah.'" Now, there is rather a spry-looking one by the door. He might be a dentist or a *masseur*. What's the muttering about in the next room?'

'Someone making a speech. Uncle Craig, most likely, as they're all trooping out. They can put up with a lot here (they have to, poor angels!), but it's only the ones who can't walk that stay and listen to Uncle Craig, and you should see the expression on their faces when they realize what they're in for—pitiful, like trapped animals!

'I heard him speak once about the peeresses in their own right who want to sit in the House of Lords. It was quite unintelligible and no wonder. His only real reason for not wanting them is that he thinks they might have to use the peers' lavatory, and, of course, he couldn't *say* that. Another time he was speaking on the Prayer Book, but somehow he got all his notes mixed up so the last half of his speech was all about new sewers for Bixton. Nobody noticed, of course, and he was able to square the reporters afterwards. Such an old duck, you know, but not exactly cut out to be a legislator.'

'It has often occurred to me to wonder, if there

26

were a revolution tomorrow, how the mob would know which were the nobles,' said Walter. 'Personally, I've always been terrified that I should be left behind when all my friends were being hurried off in the tumbrils to the echoing cry of, "*A bas les aristos!*" Never mind, I shall have my turn next day when the intelligentsia is being wiped out.'

'On the contrary, my angel, you'll hang about hoping for weeks, until at last, after all your acquaintances have died gloriously in front of Buckingham Palace or the Albert Memorial, you'll be pitched into the Thames with the other *bourgeois.*'

'Of course, it just would be one's luck. Now who'd mind going to the scaffold between Lord Lonsdale and Mrs. Meyrick! It would give one a social kick, you know. Think of the papers next day!

'"Among others I noticed on the scaffold yesterday Walter Monteath, the poet, was wearing his favourite green tie and chatting to Lord Lonsdale. He told me that his wife was busy at the moment but hopes to attend the executions to-day. Picture on back page."

'But as for all those old peers, they'll have to parade up and down Piccadilly in their coronets if they want to be taken in the smart tumbrils, and even then I expect people would think they were an advertisement for something.'

At this moment the magnificent personage strolled up to where Walter and Sally were sitting and said that Lord Craigdalloch was about to speak and if they would care to follow him he would

27

conduct them to the Strangers' Gallery, which he then proceeded to do, leading them up and down several corridors and staircases until they came to a small door, through which he pushed them into inky blackness. They groped their way to seats into which they subsided thankfully. Far below them there emerged from the gloom a sort of choked muttering.

After a few moments their eyes became more or less accustomed to the darkness and they were able to distinguish various objects—the throne, the Peeresses' Gallery, occupied by the stately figure of Lady Craigdalloch, who blew kisses to them, and two or three large tables at which some men were writing. Finally, they recognised Lord Craigdalloch. He was standing near one of the tables, and the muttering seemed to proceed from his lips. Sally was sorry, though in no way surprised, to notice that his audience consisted solely of themselves, Aunt Madge, an old bearded man seated on one of the benches with a pair of crutches just out of his reach and another stretched at full length on a red divan.

The Monteaths feverishly endeavoured to catch a few words of what their uncle was saying, but without success. As they sat straining their ears, two Frenchmen were shown into the gallery and, feeling their way to a seat, began to converse in whispers. They seemed much intrigued by the man on the divan.

'Dites donc, ce lord sur le sofa, il est saou?'
'Je dirais plutôt malade.'
'Eh bien, moi j'crois qu'il est ivre.'
'Que c'est lugubre ici.'
'Oui, rudement rasant.'

28

Lord Craigdalloch now raised his voice slightly and the words, 'the noble lord behind me . . .' were heard.

'The noble lord behind him has evidently slipped away,' murmured Sally, observing the rows of empty benches.

The old man with the beard now began to scrabble feverishly for his crutches, and finally, after a prolonged and unsuccessful effort to reach them, took off his watch-chain and lassoed one of them with it. He then hooked the other one with the crutch part and drew it towards him. Having planted them firmly under his armpits he hopped away with incredible agility, not, however, before Lord Craigdalloch had just time to say, loudly and portentously, 'My noble friend opposite.'

The departure of the only conscious member of his audience seemed now to spur him to greater vocal efforts and whole sentences could be heard at a time.

'I am convinced, m'lords, that this danger is very real. It is a very real danger. What did Scipio Africanus say?' Here he began struggling with the notes he held in his hand, but was evidently unable to find what Scipio Africanus had said. The sleeper on the divan, subconsciously aware that something was expected of him, turned rather heavily and groaned out, ''Ear! 'ear!'

'M'lords, it has been said in another place,' continued the speaker in no way put out by this slight set-back, 'that it is a very real danger. The Dukeries, m'lords, with all due respect to the noble duke behind me, are *not* to be confounded with the Fisheries. As my noble friend has so aptly remarked, it is anomalous to pretend that they are

29

analogous . . .'

Another rather younger peer now came in, sat down opposite the divan and began to read some letters.

'Enfin, on vient au secours du pauvre vieux.'

'Mais non, il n'y fait même pas attention.'

'Mon Dieu! Eh bien, voilà. C'est le flegme Britannique. Que voulez-vous? Dites donc, si on partait? Ce n'est pas follement gai ici.'

'Est-ce qu'on ôse?'

'Allons. Filons vite. Courage, mon ami.'

The Frenchmen got up and left the gallery.

At last Lord Craigdalloch made his peroration, which was quite inaudible, and sat down. The man who was reading letters sprang to his feet as though fearful of interruption (a danger, however, which hardly seemed pressing as the house was empty except for the now prostrated Craigdalloch and their sleeping compeer on the sofa), and spoke rapidly and audibly:

'M'lords, I have been asked to reply to the noble lord and I wish at the outset to express the thanks of the Government to the noble lord for so readily agreeing last May to postpone his Question, in view of the position as it then stood. At that time there was some uncertainty . . .'

Here Lady Craigdalloch leant over the rail of the Peeresses' Gallery and by a series of signals gave the Monteaths to understand that she was ready to go and would meet them outside.

When, after losing their way once or twice, they at last reached the Princes Chamber, they found her waiting there for them. A tall commanding woman with white hair and an Edwardian aspect, she had, in the days when big pale faces and Grecian features

30

were admired to the exclusion of everything else, been considered a beauty. She had still considerable remains of looks and the unmistakable manner of one who has been courted in youth and flattered in middle-age.

'Dear Sally,' she said, embracing her niece rather voluminously, 'I knew you would like to hear your uncle's speech. It went off very well, didn't it? Always such an anxiety to the dear thing. How well you are looking, Sally. Where did you get so wonderfully sunburnt?'

'At Elizabeth Arden's, Aunt Madge.'

Lady Craigdalloch inwardly supposed that this must be one of Walter's Bright Young but Undesirable friends that she was always hearing so much about from Sally's mother. The creature probably has a villa in the South of France—so much the better, those sort of people are not wanted in England, where they merely annoy their elders and breed Socialism. In any case, she never understood this craving of the younger generation for a hideous brick-coloured complexion. If she had guessed for a moment that Sally stained hers every morning with stuff out of a bottle she would have thought her niece frankly mad.

'Craig will join us in a moment. He wishes us to begin tea without him.' She led the way down long, draughty, Gothic corridors to the tea-room, which, in contrast to other portions of the House, presented a scene of tempestuous gaiety. Several of the peers seated at the rather *intime* little tables were considerably under seventy, and one or two had relations and female friends with them whom they were entertaining with jokes and witticisms of the most abandoned description. Two bishops and

31

some of their girl friends were fairly rollicking over a pot of tea, while the old man with crutches was being jocularly accused by the Lord Chancellor of having wiped his beard on the table-cloth, an allegation which he could hardly refute, having been caught by that dignitary in the very act. Altogether there was a spirit of goodwill and friendly banter which seemed more or less lacking elsewhere in the building.

While Walter and Sally were eating the fascinating mixed biscuits and strong tea which the nation, through the medium of Richard Coeur de Maison Lyons, provides at a slight profit for the sustenance of its administrators and their guests, Lady Craigdalloch explained in what their duties at Dalloch Castle would consist.

'You will find everything running very smoothly. I think. The servants have all been there for years and you'll have no trouble at all with them. You will, of course, give any orders for the comfort of the guests, such as, for instance, how many picnic luncheons will be required for the guns, and so on. Then, if you would meet the new arrivals in the hall and show them their rooms, that sort of thing makes people feel so much more at home than if they arrive and find no host or hostess.'

'When would you like us to go up there?' asked Sally.

'Let me think. The first guests, of course, arrive on the 10th. Could you go up about the 8th? You'll find General Murgatroyd. He's there now, dear thing, fishing.'

'Is it a big party for the 12th?'

'I think I can tell you exactly who will be there. Lord and Lady Prague—he is a great friend of your papa, Sally; very deaf, poor dear, but an extremely good shot. He married her *en secondes noces* some years ago. She was Florence Graiday. She will be a great help to you, I think, a wonderfully charming woman and so artistic. They will probably stay quite a month. They always do every year. Then a delightful couple, the Chadlingtons. Brenda Chadlington is the daughter of a very old friend of mine. She is a most beautiful creature. The other two guns are Admiral Wenceslaus, a dear thing with only one eye; and Mr. Buggins, who is, of course, secretary of the Nelson Club, a very cultured man. His wife, poor woman, is shut up, has been quite mad for years.'

'Is General Murgatroyd married?' asked Sally rather nervously. She felt that all these women might prove to be very alarming.

'No, dear, he is not. That is to say, he *was* married but unfortunately, he was obliged to divorce his wife. None of us was surprised. She was a girl from the Baker Street Bazaar, you know. She got a hold over him somehow and made him marry her. But it all happened years ago—thirty years at least, I suppose. Here comes your Uncle Craig.'

Sally kissed her uncle, who seemed genuinely pleased to see her.

'We heard your speech, Uncle Craig,' she lied, 'from the Strangers' Gallery. It was most interesting.'

'Glad you think so, my dear. One has one's duty, you know; born into a certain position and so forth. It's no use pretending that one enjoys coming here, or that it will be very pleasant going off to New South Rhodesia just when the moor has never been better. Still, as my poor father used to say, one's not only put here for enjoyment. All the same,' he added, brightening somewhat, 'Gillibrough tells me I may get the chance of shooting a lion or two and possibly some hartebeest in Rhodesia. Well, Walter, what d'you think of this place? Never been here before, eh? Finest legislative assembly in the world, you know, nothing to touch it anywhere. Made England what she is to-day—the House of Lords. The work that goes on here, you wouldn't believe it. There's no place like it for work, and all unpaid. And then the Socialists pretend we don't do our bit. I'll tell you one thing, Walter: the reform of the House of Lords will be the downfall of England.' He bristled at the idea, then continued more gently, 'So you two are going up to Dalloch to look after our guests for us, eh? Very kind of you, I think. Now, have you any friends of your own you'd like to ask for the shooting, eh?'

'We'd rather like to ask someone called Albert Gates, if we may, but he doesn't shoot, I'm afraid.'

'Doesn't shoot? And Walter doesn't shoot either? I can't think what all these young men are coming to. What does he do, then?'

'He studies painting, Uncle Craig.'

'An artist, is he? Well, well, how did you get to know him, then? As a matter of fact, now I come to think of it, I once knew an artist myself called Leighton—Lord Leighton. Not a bad fellow at all, really quite a decent sort of chap considering. If your friend paints he'll like being up at Dalloch: the views are really superb, wonderful colour effects, you know.'

'The old parts of the house are very paintable too,' said Lady Craigdalloch. 'Dear Mr. Buggins always does some charming water-colour sketches

34

on non-shooting days.'

'See that youngish man who's just come in, Sally?' said her uncle suddenly.

Sally saw a man of unbelievable age creeping towards them, his limbs positively shaking with palsy.

'That's Prague, he's going to be at Dalloch with you. You'd better meet him. Here, Prague! (He's very deaf so speak up, won't you?) *Prague, this is my niece, Mrs. Monteath. She's going to be at Dalloch.*'

Lord Prague gave her a gouty hand and said in a quavering voice:

'You must be Johnnie's daughter, I suppose. Now, how is Johnnie?'

'*Not very well,*' screamed Sally. '*He's doing a cure at Baden.*'

'I'm very sorry to hear it. A young man like Johnnie should not be doing cures yet. Why, it's only yesterday he was my fag at Eton. Cure be damned! Little Johnnie. Yes, he was Captain of the Boats—only yesterday! Well, see you in Scotland, I hope. I must go now. They may divide on this. Coming, Craig?'

★   ★   ★

Walter and Sally, on their return home, found Albert talking to Jane Dacre, Sally's greatest and, indeed, only woman friend.

'Jane, dear, how nice to see you! Did you know Albert before? Anyhow, I'm glad to see he gave you a cocktail.'

'No, we've never met before, and in point of fact, I gave him one. He didn't seem to know where the drinks are kept.'

35

'I have been telling Miss Dacre about our party last night,' said Albert. 'What have you two been doing this afternoon?'

'We have been visiting the greatest legislative assembly in the world, namely, the House of Lords, and one of the legislators took such a fancy to us that he has lent us a castle and a grouse moor in Scotland for two months. And this is a perfectly true fact, believe me or not as you like, but please both come and stay and bring your guns.'

Sally explained the circumstances.

'You must both come and help us with these Pragues and Murgatroyds and people. There's an admiral with one eye and a man with a lunatic wife, but he's not bringing her because she's in a loony bin. So do come, angels, won't you?'

Albert accepted without any hesitation.

'I have never been to Scotland,' he said, 'which, for an earnest student of the Victorian era, is a very serious admission. I am happy to think that I shall soon see with my own eyes and in such charming company, that scenery of bens and braes which is so impregnated with the nineteenth century. It is also a unique chance, as I am told that no cultured people ever go there now, so much is it *démodé*.'

'I'd love to come, too,' said Jane, 'if I may let you know for certain in the morning. I shall have to ask the family—but I expect they'll be delighted. There is something so very respectable about Scotland.'

CHAPTER FIVE

Jane Dacre sat in the restaurant car of the Scotch express about a month later. She had accepted Sally's invitation with great pleasure and her family's full consent, and was much looking forward to the visit, partly because she would thus avoid seeing her parents for a whole month, but chiefly because she was devoted to Walter and Sally, and rather in love with Albert.

Jane was a very ordinary sort of girl, but her character, as is so often the case with women, manifested itself by a series of contradictions and was understood by nobody. Thought by some to be exceptionally stupid, and by others brilliantly clever, she was in reality neither. She had certain talents which she was far too lazy to develop, and a sort of feminine astuteness that prevented her from saying silly things. Like many women she had taste without much intellect, her brain was like a mirror, reflecting the thoughts and ideas of her more intelligent friends and the books that she read. Although she was able to perceive originality in others, she was herself completely unoriginal. She had, however, a sense of humour, and except for a certain bitterness with which, for no apparent reason, she regarded her mother and father, the temperament of an angel.

Her attitude towards her parents was, indeed, very curious. She always spoke of them as though they were aged half-wits with criminal tendencies, whose one wish was to render her life miserable. Those of her friends who had met them never could account for this. They were charming, rather cultured people, obviously devoted to their only child, and Jane when she was actually with them seemed to return their devotion. That she was a great trial to them there could be no doubt. Men fell easily in love with her, and she was usually having an affair with some really unsuitable person. As she was most indiscreet she had acquired, among people of her parents' generation, a very bad reputation, which was hardly deserved. Up to the present she had not been married, having a sort of vague idea in her head that she wished to be the wife of a genius. In the same way that some girls will not marry for love alone but must have money too, only allowing themselves to fall in love with a millionaire, so Jane thought that she could never be happy except with a really clever man; she had little intellect of her own, and needed the constant stimulus of an intellectual companion.

She had intended to marry when and only when she had found the ideal person, but she was in no hurry. The idea rather bored her, and the example of her married friends (except for Walter and Sally) was, to say the least of it, unpromising.

Meanwhile, she fell in love right and left, and had many violent but short-lived love affairs, in the course of which she burnt her own fingers comparatively seldom.

The train was full of sportsmen, their wives and dogs, going North. The most depressing sight in the world, thought Jane, is a married couple travelling. The horror of it. Not only must they sleep, eat, walk, drive and go to the theatre together all their lives, but they cannot escape even in the train. It brings home to one what marriage really means more than anything else, except perhaps seeing a married couple at the bridge table. What is the terrifying chain which binds these wretched people together so inevitably? Love? Hardly, or they would look happier. Intellectual companionship? No, that certainly not; the misery on their faces is only exceeded by the boredom. Habit and convention, no doubt, aided by the natural slavishness of women. Probably they are too stupid to realize their own unhappiness. They all look terribly, terribly stupid.

As Jane glanced around, her attention was particularly attracted by one couple who seemed rather different from the rest, and yet in a way typical of them all.

The husband was an example of sporting Englishman to be seen by the dozen on every race-course and with whom the Embassy is nightly packed. He was tall, rather burly, with a phenomenally small head, mouse-coloured hair and reddish moustache. Although possessing almost classical features he was as ugly an object as could be imagined.

His wife was more unusual looking. She was immensely long and thin, so that she appeared, as it were, out of drawing, like an object seen in a distorting mirror. Her face, terribly thin and haggard, was completely dominated by an enormously long thin nose which turned up slightly at the very end: her large dark eyes were set close together and looked short-sighted. Her mouth was simply a red line, showing up startlingly on her dead white skin with green shadows. Jane thought that she had never seen anyone look so much like an overbred horse. She even ate like one, appearing to sniff every mouthful cautiously before she allowed herself to nibble at it, as though she might at any moment shy away from the table. Her husband behaved to her just like a groom with a nervous mare. Jane felt that he must have had difficulty in accustoming her to being handled.

She was well-dressed in an English sort of way; her tweeds were perfectly cut, and everything she wore was obviously expensive. Beautiful rings gave the uncomfortable impression of being too big for her fingers, which were abnormally thin and nervous. Her pearls were real. She wore a regimental badge of diamonds and rubies on a thick crêpe de chine jumper. While lacking any real *chic*, she gave an impression of genuineness and worth so unusual as to be rather pleasant. The word 'bogus' would under no circumstances have applied to her.

Jane, who was clever with her own clothes, felt annoyed with the long thin woman who, she thought, might have made more of her appearance without in any way detracting from its originality. 'And is it necessary to look as bored as that?' Jane wondered. Of course, the husband was most uninspiring, but still she might look out of the window sometimes, or at her fellow-passengers instead of staring into space in that almost loopy way. Perhaps she had a hidden life of her own into which she could retire at will, or possibly she was in fact as stupid as she looked. Jane hoped for her sake that this was so.

At last she turned to her husband and said something. Only her lips moved, the expression of her face was unchanged. He nodded. Presently he gave her a cigarette and she began to blow the

40

smoke through her nostrils like a horse in the cold weather.

Jane paid her bill and wandered back to her third-class sleeper. When she reached it she stood for a few moments in the corridor looking out of the windows at sunny fields with immense shadows of trees and hedges lying across them. The setting sun made a yellow mist over everything.

'By the time I get back to England, autumn will have begun,' she thought vaguely. Her mind was full of Albert Gates.

Jane's love affairs generally consisted of three phases. During the first phase—which lasted over a length of time varying with the number of meetings, but not often exceeding two months—she was violently in love. When away from the object of her affections she would think of him constantly in a light which generally bore a very small relation to truth; when in his company she would force herself to be happy, although she was often disillusioned in little ways. The second phase was complicated, but rendered more exciting by the reciprocation of her feelings. This seldom lasted for very long, as the third phase, consisting of heartless, but determined backing out on the part of Jane, would almost immediately follow. The first and second phases were generally accompanied by shameful flirtation.

At the present moment Jane was undergoing the usual preliminary phase with regard to Albert. She had met him several times in London and thought him easily the most attractive person of her acquaintance. As she gazed out of the corridor window it occurred to her that here, most probably, was the genius for whom she had been searching for such a long time; her brain circled, as it were, round and round the subject, but she sought no

41

conclusion and arrived at none. Presently the long thin woman passed by on her way to the first-class sleepers, followed by her husband. In motion she looked more than ever like a horse.

Jane climbed into her sleeper and lay down. She was sharing the carriage with three other women, all, luckily, unknown to each other, so there was no conversation. They looked at her with some disapproval as, contrary to third-class convention, she undressed completely and put on a pair of pyjamas. She greased her face, brushed her hair and settled down for a horrible night of banging, jolting and waking up at countless stations. All the time she half thought, half dreamed of Albert, wondering if he would have arrived yet at Dalloch Castle, how long he intended to stay, and whether he was at all excited at the prospect of their meeting. Towards the morning she fell into a profound sleep.

When she woke up the train was passing through Highland scenery. Purple hills kept rising outside the carriage window and obscuring the sky. They were covered with little streams and sheep. Everything was very quiet, even the train seemed to make less noise than it had done the previous evening; the air had a peculiar quality of extreme clearness like cold water.

Jane felt, but quickly checked, a romantic tremor. She removed her gaze from the moors and began to dress. The other women were still asleep, looking like modern German pictures.

At Inverness, Jane had to change into a local train, which ambled for about an hour in rather an intimate sort of way over moors and through pine woods, stopping here and there at little toy stations.

When she alighted at Dalloch Station she noticed the long thin woman of the previous night standing by the guard's van with her husband, and presumed that they must be going to the castle. Sure enough, when they had collected their luggage, which took some time because there was a great deal of it as well as two spaniels, they climbed into the motor-car where Jane was already installed and introduced themselves as the Chadlingtons. She gathered from labels on their hand luggage that they were Captain and Lady Brenda Chadlington, a name she seemed vaguely to know.

'Have you stayed at Dalloch before?' asked Lady Brenda as they drove out of the station yard.

'No; you see, I don't know the Craigdallochs. Sally Monteath asked me. Have you been here before?'

'Oh, yes! Every year since I can remember. Madge Craigdalloch is my mother's greatest friend and my godmother. I can't imagine what it will be like without her and Craig, although I'm told the Monteaths are charming. What bad luck for poor Craig having to go off like that, wasn't it . . . ?'

She rambled on in the bored, uninterested voice of one who has been taught to think any conversation is better than none. Her husband looked out of the window in silence.

CHAPTER SIX

Sally greeted them in the hall of Dalloch Castle on their arrival. She was looking lovelier than usual in a pair of pink satin pyjamas.

43

'Please excuse these clothes. I've just this moment woken up. We only got here last night after a most fiendish journey in the car. How tired you must all be. I've had hot-water bottles put in your beds and breakfast will be sent up at once. Shall we go upstairs?'

The Chadlingtons glanced at each other in a startled kind of way.

General Murgatroyd now appeared and was introduced to Jane. He evidently knew the Chadlingtons very well and offered to show them their rooms, while Sally, relieved to have got rid of them, carried off Jane to have breakfast with herself and Walter, who was still in bed.

'Let's fetch old Gates,' said Walter, 'and have a party in here.'

Sally turned on the gramophone while he went along the passage, soon to return with Albert, who looked sleepy but cheerful in a pair of orange pyjamas. Jane thought him more attractive even than in London.

Presently trays of delicious breakfast appeared and they all sat on the bed munching happily, except Albert who announced that he was unable to touch food in the morning and asked the slightly astonished housemaid for a glass of Maraschino.

Jane asked if he had also travelled up in the Craigdallochs' car.

'Indeed, yes,' he replied. 'What a journey, too; all through England's green unpleasant land, as Blake so truly calls it. My one happy moment was at Carlisle, where we spent a night. When I opened what I supposed to be a cupboard door in my room, I was greeted by inky blackness, through which was just visible a pile of sordid clothes and cries of:

44

"Well, I'm damned!" and "What impertinence!" It was a conjugal bedroom!'

Jane laughed.

'I expect if you knew the truth it was no such thing.'

'Well, I thought of that myself, but came to the conclusion that people who were indulging in a little enjoyable sin would probably be in better tempers. They actually rang the bell and said very loudly to the maid so that I couldn't fail to hear: "The person next door *keeps* coming in. Will you please lock it on this side so that we can have some peace?" *Keeps coming in*, indeed, as though I wanted to know the details of their squalid *ménage*. However, I had my revenge. I cleaned my teeth very loudly every half-hour all through the night. It woke them up each time, too! I could hear them grumbling.'

'Has all the rest of the party arrived?' asked Jane.

'All except Lord and Lady Prague. The general, whom you saw downstairs, Admiral Wenceslaus and Mr. Buggins were all here last night,' said Walter. 'We had about half an hour's conversation with them before going to bed. Mr. Buggins seems rather nice and Sally has quite fallen for the admiral.'

'As I have for the general,' remarked Albert; 'but then I have always had a great *penchant* for soldiers. It fascinates me to think how brave they must be. Sometimes one sees them marching about in London, all looking so wonderfully brave. I admire that. Sailors, too, must be very courageous, but somehow one doesn't feel it in quite the same way. Perhaps the fact that they are clean-shaven makes them more akin to oneself. This particular admiral

45

certainly fixed upon me an extremely fierce and penetrating eye; instinctively I thought here is the hero of many an ocean fight, a rare old sea-dog.'

'His eye,' said Walter, 'is glass. At least, one of them is. I don't want to disillusion you, Albert dear.'

'How fascinating!' cried Albert. 'I knew the moment I saw him that the admiral was not quite as we are. This accounts for it. How d'you think he lost it, Walter? I suppose it hardly could have been plucked out by pirates or the Inquisition? Do you think he is sensitive about it? Will he, for instance, mind if he sees me looking closely at him to discover which eye is which? I must find out how he lost it. I suppose it would be tactless to ask him right out? But the general may know. I don't despair. Or Mr. Buggins. I like Mr. Buggins. He appears to be a man of some culture. He saw my picture "Tape Measures" reproduced in the *Studio* and was kind enough to mention it appreciatively.

'Now, my dears, I am going to dress, as I can hardly wait to begin exploring this house, which promises, in my opinion, to be very rewarding to the intelligent student of the nineteenth century. What do you intend to put on, Walter? I fear I have no tweeds, so shall be obliged to wear some trousers and a jersey. Will that be suitable, do you think?'

He picked up his black taffeta wrap and left the room.

★　　★　　★

Meanwhile, General Murgatroyd escorted the Chadlingtons to the dining-room where they made a hearty breakfast of sausages, eggs, ham and strong

46

tea. The general, who some two hours since had eaten enough for three, kept them company with a plate of brawn. They all spoke in monosyllables, their mouths full.

'Bad luck for poor old Craig.'

'Oh, rotten.'

'When did the Monteaths get here?'

'Last night—late.'

'Anybody else?'

'Stanislas is here and Buggins.'

'Anybody else?'

'Yes; namby-pamby chap called Gates—artist or something. Came with the Monteaths.'

'Who's to come?'

'Only Floss and Prague. Coming to-night.'

'Does Monteath shoot?'

'No, nor Gates. Just as well, from the look of them.'

'What's Mrs. Monteath like?'

'Oh, all right. Better than the others, I should say.'

'Pretty, isn't she?'

'Too much dolled up for me, otherwise quite handsome.'

'Finished your breakfast?'

'M'm!'

'Come and look at the river, then.'

'Wait a moment. We'll get our rods put up.'

'Not much use, too bright.'

'Oh, we might as well have a try, all the same.'

★   ★   ★

About two hours later, Jane, having bathed and changed out of her travelling clothes, wandered downstairs, where she came upon Albert, exquisitely dressed in bright blue trousers and a black sweater. He was roaming about, notebook in hand.

'My dear Jane,' he said, 'this house is unique. I am in ecstasies. Most of it seems scarcely to have been touched for the last fifty years. Nevertheless, we are only just in time. The hand of the modern decorator is already upon it. The drawing-room, alas! I find utterly ruined. Our absent hostess would appear to have that Heal *cum* Lenigen complex so prevalent among the British aristocracy. Happily, in this case, it has been muzzled, presumably by lack of funds, but its influence is creeping over the whole house. The oak, for instance, on these stairs and in the entrance hall has been pickled—a modern habit, which one cannot too heartily deplore—and much exquisite furniture has been banished to the servants' hall, some even to the attics. On the other hand, the boudoir, stone hall, billiard- and dining-rooms appear to be quite unspoilt. Come with me, my dear.'

Albert led the way to the dining-room, where the table was being laid for luncheon. It was a huge room with dark red brocade walls and a pale blue-and-yellow ceiling covered in real gold stars. At one end there arose an enormous Gothic mantelpiece of pitch-pine. Several Raeburns and two Winterhalters adorned the walls.

'Winterhalter,' murmured Albert, 'my favourite artist. I must call your attention to this clock, made of the very cannon-ball which rolled to the feet of Ernest, 4th Earl of Craigdalloch during the battle of Inkerman. Shall we go and look at the outside of the castle? We have just time before lunch.'

48

They went into the garden and walked around the house, which was built in the Victorian feudal style, and rather resembled a large white cake with windows and battlements picked out in chocolate icing. Albert was thrown into raptures by its appearance.

When they returned to the front door they found Walter and the general standing on the steps.

'Ah! this house! this house!' cried Albert. 'I am enchanted by it. Good morning, General.'

'Good morning, Gates.'

'Walter, have you ever seen such a house? General, you agree, I hope, that it is truly exquisite?'

'Yes; I am attached to the place myself. Been here, man and boy, for the last fifty years or so. Best grouse moor in the country, you know, and as good fishing as you can find between here and the Dee, I swear it is.'

'It *is* lovely,' said Jane doubtfully. 'I wonder what we shall do all day though.'

'Do? Why, my dear young lady, by the time you've been out with the guns, or flogging the river all day, you'll be too tired to do anything except perhaps to have a set or two of lawn tennis. After dinner we can always listen to Craig's wireless. I've just asked the chauffeur to fix it up.'

'I personally shall be busy taking photographs,' said Albert. 'I am shortly bringing out a small brochure on the minor arts of the nineteenth century, and although I had already collected much material for it, there are in this house some objects so unique that I shall have to make a most careful revision of my little work. I also feel it is my duty to the nation to compile a catalogue of what I find

49

here. You write, General?'

'I once wrote a series of articles for *Country Life* on stable bedding.'

'But how macabre! Then you, I and Walter, all three, belong to the fellowship of the pen; but while you and I are in a way but tyros, I feeling frankly more at home with a paintbrush and you, most probably, with a fox's brush, Walter here is one of our latter day immortals.'

And he bagan to recite in a loud voice one of his friend's poems:

'*Fallow upon the great black waste*
'*And all esurient. But when*
'*Your pale green tears are falling*
Falling   and
Falling
Upon the Wapentake, there was never
So absolutely never
Such disparity.'

Walter blushed.

'*Please*, Albert.'

'My dear Walter, that is good. It is more than good—it has an enduring quality and I think will live. Do you not agree, general? You and I, Walter, will do a great deal of work here. I have found a room with a large green table in the centre very well lighted. It will be ideal for my purpose. Then I am hoping that Sally will perhaps give me a few sittings. Do you think that she might be persuaded?'

'My dear, she'd adore to. Sally very much believes in having herself reproduced in all mediums. Come on. There's the gong for lunch.'

50

*　　　*　　　*

By dinner-time that evening the whole party was assembled, Lord and Lady Prague having arrived in a motorcar soon after seven o'clock.

Sally had spent much time and thought over the arrangement of the table, feeling that it was her duty to try and make the first evening a success, and as she sat down she thought, with some satisfaction, that she had mixed up the party rather well. It soon became apparent, however, that the party was not mixing. Her own task, seated between Lord Prague and Captain Chadlington, might well have daunted a far more experienced conversationalist, the former being stone deaf and moreover thoroughly engrossed in the pleasures of the table, while the latter appeared to possess a vocabulary of exactly three words—'I say!' and 'No!'—which he used alternately. She fought a losing battle valiantly, remembering that the really important thing on these occasions is to avoid an oasis of silence. Walter declared afterwards that he distinctly heard her ask Lord Prague if he belonged to the London Group, and that, on receiving no answer, she then proceeded to recite *Lycidas* to him until the end of dinner.

Jane, whose partners were Admiral Wenceslaus and Mr. Buggins, courted disaster by embarking on a funny story Albert had told her about a lunatic woman with a glass eye. She only remembered in the middle that the admiral was one-eyed and that Mrs. Buggins languished in a lunatic asylum and had to change it quickly into a drunken man with one leg. The story lost much of its point and

51

nobody laughed except Walter, who choked into his soup.

Albert sat next to Lady Prague, a spinsterish woman of about forty with a fat face, thin body and the remains of a depressingly insular type of good looks. Her fuzzy brown hair was arranged in a dusty bun showing ears which were evidently intended to be hidden, but which insisted on poking their way out. Her skin was yellow with mauve powder; except for this her face was quite free from any trace of *maquillage*, and the eyebrows grew at will. Her nails were cut short and unvarnished.

Albert was seized with spasms of hatred for her even before she spoke, which she did almost immediately in a loud unpleasing voice, saying:

'I didn't quite hear your name when we were introduced.'

Albert looked at her frolicking eyebrows with distaste and said very distinctly:

'Albert Memorial Gates.'

'Oh! What?'

'Albert Memorial Gates.'

'Yes. *Memorial*, did you say?'

'My name,' said Albert with some asperity, 'is Albert Memorial Gates. I took Memorial in addition to my baptismal Albert at my confirmation out of admiration for the Albert Memorial, a very great work of art which may be seen in a London suburb called Kensington.'

'Oh,' said Lady Prague crossly, 'you might as well have called yourself Albert Hall.'

'I entirely disagree with you.'

Lady Prague looked helplessly at her other neighbour, Admiral Wenceslaus, but he was talking

52

across Jane to Mr. Buggins and took no notice of her. She made the best of a bad job and turned again to Albert.

'Did I hear Mr. Buggins say that you are an artist?'

'*Artiste—peintre*—yes.'

'Oh, now do tell me, I'm so interested in art, what do you chiefly go in for?'

'Go in where?'

'I mean—water-colours or oils?'

'My principal medium is what you would call oils. Gouache, tempera and prepared dung are mediums I never neglect, while my bead, straw and button pictures have aroused a great deal of criticism not by any means all unfavourable.'

'It always seems to me a great pity to go in for oils unless you're really good. Now Prague's sister has a girl who draws quite nicely and she wanted to go on to Paris, but I said to her parents, "Why let her learn oils. There are too many oil paintings in the world already. Let her do water-colours. They take up much less room." Don't you agree?'

'I expect, in the case of your husband's niece, that you were perfectly right.'

'Now, do tell me, this is so interesting, what sort of things do you paint?'

'Chiefly abstract subjects.'

'Yes, I see, allegories and things like that. Art must be so fascinating, I always think. I have just been painted by Laszlo. By the way, did I see you at his exhibition? No? But I have seen you somewhere before, I know I have. It's a funny thing but I *never* forget a face—names, now I can't remember, but I never forget a face, do you?'

'So few people have faces,' said Albert, who was

53

struggling to be polite. 'Everyone seems to have a name, but only one person in ten has a face. The old man sitting next to Sally, for instance, has no face at all.'

'That is my husband,' said Lady Prague, rather tartly.

'Then the fact must already have obtruded itself on your notice. But, take the general as an example. He hasn't got one either, in my opinion.'

'Oh, I see now what you mean,' she said brightly, 'that they are not paintable. But you surprise me. I have always been told that older people, especially men, were very paintable with all the wrinkles and lines—so much character. Now you went, I suppose, to the Dutch exhibition?'

'I did not. I wasn't in London last spring, as a matter of fact, but even if I had been I should have avoided Burlington House as sedulously then as I should later in the summer. I regard the Dutch school as one of the many sins against art which have been perpetrated through the ages.'

'You mean . . .' She looked at him incredulously. 'Don't you *like* Dutch pictures?'

'No, nor Dutch cheese, as a matter of fact!'

'I can't understand it. I simply worship them. There was a picture of an old woman by Rembrandt. I stood in front of it for quite a while one day and I *could have sworn* she breathed!'

Albert shuddered.

'Yes, eerie, wasn't it? I turned to my friend and said: "Laura, it's uncanny. I feel she might step out of the frame any moment." Laura Pastille (Mrs. Pastille, that's my friend's name) has copied nearly all the Dutch pictures in the National Gallery. For some she had to use a magnifying glass. She's very

54

artistic. But I am amazed that you don't like them. I suppose you pretend to admire all these ugly things which are the fashion now. I expect you'll get over it in time. Epstein, for instance, and Augustus John—what d'you think about them?'

Albert contained himself with some difficulty and answered, breathing hard and red in the face, that he regarded Epstein as one of the great men of all time and would prefer not to discuss him. (General Murgatroyd, overhearing this remark, turned to Walter and asked if that 'fella Gates' were an aesthete. Walter looked puzzled and said that he hoped so, he hoped they all were. The general snorted and continued telling Captain Chadlington about how he had once played a salmon for two hours.)

Lady Prague then said: 'Why do you live in Paris? Isn't England good enough for you?' She said this rather offensively. It was evident that Albert's feelings for her were heartily reciprocated.

'Well,' he replied, 'England is hardly a very good place for a serious artist, is it? One is not exactly encouraged to use one's brain over here, you know. When I arrived from Paris this last time they would not even leave me my own copy of *Ulysses*. Things have come to a pretty pass when it is impossible to get decent literature to read.'

'*In*decent literature, I suppose you mean.'

Albert felt completely out of his depth, but to his immense relief Admiral Wenceslaus now turned upon Lady Prague the conversational gambit of, 'And where did you come from today?' thus making it unnecessary for him to answer.

Mr. Buggins and Walter were getting on like a house on fire.

55

'Curious,' observed Mr. Buggins, 'for a house party of this size in Scotland to consist entirely of Sassenachs—seven men and not one kilt among them. I have the right, of course, to wear the Forbes tartan through my maternal grandmother, but I always think it looks bad with an English name, don't you agree?'

'Very bad,' said Walter. 'But you could wear it as a fancy dress, I suppose?'

'The kilt, my dear sir, is not a fancy dress.'

'My wife is Scottish; her father is Lord Craigdalloch's brother.'

'Yes, of course, Johnnie. Such an interesting family, the Dallochs; one of the oldest in Scotland.'

'Really?'

'Considering that you are allied to them by marriage it surprises me that you should not be aware of that. Why, the cellars of this castle date from the tenth century. I suppose you know how it came to be built here?'

'I'm afraid I don't.'

'Well, the first Thane of Dalloch had no castle and one day when he was getting old he thought he would build himself a solid dwelling-place instead of the shieling or hut that had been his headquarters up to then. So he went to consult a wise woman who lived in a neighbouring shieling. He told her what was in his mind and asked where would be the best place for him to build his castle. She replied, "When you find a *bike* [*wasps' nest*] in a *birk* [*birch tree*], *busk* [*prepare*] there the *bauk* [*cross beam*]."'

'The story goes that as he was walking away from the old woman's shieling he was stung by a wasp. He looked high and low for the *bike*, intending to destroy it, and presently found it in a *birk*. Instantly

56

he recalled the witch's words. The next day he *busked* the *bauk* and soon a bonnie castle rose round the *birk*, which you can see to this very day in the cellars. To me, all these old legends are so fascinating.'

He then proceeded to tell Walter the whole history of the Dalloch family down to the present generation. Walter found it extremely dull and wondcrcd how anyonc could bc bothcrcd to remember such stuff, but he thought Mr. Buggins quite a nice old bore and tried to listen intelligently.

Albert was now struggling with Lady Brenda, who was far more difficult to get on with than Lady Prague. Being a duke's daughter she was always spoken of as having so much charm. The echo of this famous charm had even reached as far as Paris, and Albert was eagerly anticipating its influence upon himself.

He was doomed to immediate disappointment, finding that besides being an unusually stupid woman she had less sex appeal than the average cauliflower; and when, in the course of conversation, he learnt that her two children were called Wendy and Christopher Robin, his last hope of being charmed vanished for ever.

She told him that Lady Craigdalloch, her godmother, was improving the whole house, bit by bit.

'This year all the oak on the staircase has been pickled. Of course, it takes time as they are not well off, but Madge has such good taste. You should have seen the drawing-room before she redecorated it: a hideous white room with nothing but Victorian furniture, bead stools and those horrible little stiff sofas. It was my mother who suggested painting it

57

green. Of course it is really lovely now.'

'You have known the house a long time?' he asked, stifling a groan.

'Oh, yes, since I was a child. We spent our honeymoon here.'

'I hope,' said Albert, 'in the lovely bed which Sally is occupying at present. I thought when I saw it how perfect for a honeymoon.'

Lady Brenda looked horrified. Luckily at this moment Sally got up and the women left the dining-room.

As soon as the door was shut upon them, Admiral Wenceslaus monopolized the conversation, holding forth on his favourite subject: Blockade. Walter and Albert, who had a hazy idea that a blockade was a sort of fence behind which the white men retired when pursued by Red Indians, now learnt that, on the contrary, it is a system of keeping supplies from the enemy in times of war. The admiral explained to them, and to the table at large, that it is permissible to ration neutrals to their pre-war imports in order to prevent the enemy country from importing goods through this channel.

'Why wasn't it done from the beginning?' he bawled, in a voice which Albert felt he must have acquired when addressing his men in stormy weather from the bridge, and rolling his eye round and round. 'Was there a traitor in the Government? That's what I should like to know.'

'Hear, hear!' said Lord Prague, doubtless from force of habit, as he was, in fact, unable to hear a word.

'We had them *there*.' The admiral screwed his thumb round and round on the table as though grinding up imaginary Germans. 'And all the time

58

our poor fellows were being blown to atoms by British shells...'

His speech, for it was virtually one, continued for about half an hour, and when it was finished they joined the ladies.

Albert felt disappointed. Other admirals he had met had provided excellent after-dinner company and he expected better things of the Silent Service than a lecture on Blockade.

CHAPTER SEVEN

After dinner the general marshalled them all into Lord Craigdalloch's study and turned on the wireless which was playing Grieg's suite from *Peer Gynt*. 'This is London calling.' (Crash! crash!) 'The Wireless Symphony Orchestra will now play "Solveig's Song."' (Crash! crash! crash!)

Albert spoke to Jane in an undertone, but he was quickly checked by a look from Lady Prague who appeared to be in a state of aesthetic rapture.

When the Grieg came to an end it was announced that Miss Sackville-West would give readings from T. S. Eliot.

'Tripe!' said the general and turned it off. He then began to arrange about the next day's shooting.

'If any of the non-shooters would like to come out tomorrow,' he said, 'it will be a good opportunity as none of the drives are very far apart and it's all easy walking. Those who don't want to come all day can meet us for lunch.'

'Jane and I would love it if we shan't be in the

59

way,' said Sally meekly.

The general, who had taken a fancy to her, smiled benignly:

'Do you good, my dear.'

'Great,' said Albert, 'as is my distaste for natural scenery, I feel it to be my duty, as a student of the nineteenth century, to gaze just once upon the glens and bens that so entranced Royal Victoria, both as the happy wife of that industrious and illustrious prince whose name I am so proud to bear, and as his lamenting relict. I should like to see the stag stand at bay upon its native crags, the eagle cast its great shadow over the cowering grouse; I should like dearly to find a capercailzie's nest. And I feel that I could choose no more suitable day on which to witness these glories of Victorian nature than the famous twelfth, when sportsmen all over the country set forth with dog and gun to see what they can catch.'

This speech was greeted by Captain Chadlington with a sort of admiring noise in his throat which can only be transcribed as 'Co-o-o-h'

'Shall you come, Monteath?' asked the general, taking no notice of Albert.

'I think not, sir, thank you very much. I have rather a lot of work to do for the *Literary Times* and if everyone goes out it will be a good opportunity to get on with it.'

'Brenda and I will come, of course,' said Lady Prague briskly, 'so we shall be five extra beside the guns. Will you ring the bell, Mowbray?' The general did so. She added, with a disapproving look at Albert: 'Don't you shoot?'

'Excellently,' he replied in a threatening voice. 'With the water-pistol.'

60

'Perhaps you had no chance of learning when you were young; probably you have a good *natural* eye.'

The admiral looked annoyed and there was an awkward silence.

'Well, then,' said General Murgatroyd, 'that's all settled. Those who are coming out in the morning must be in the hall, suitably dressed, by ten. We shan't wait. I advise you to bring shooting-sticks.'

'What are they?' asked Albert, but his question was drowned by the overture from *William Tell* which suddenly burst upon the room.

*   *   *

The next day Jane came downstairs punctually at ten o'clock. Albert and Sally had apparently both found themselves unable to get up so early and had sent messages to say that they would join the guns for lunch. One of the footmen was just taking a glass of champagne to Albert's room. Jane wished that she had known this sooner; she had found it a great effort to wake up that morning herself, and was still very sleepy. She half contemplated going back to bed until luncheon time, but catching at that moment the eye of the admiral, and feeling by no means certain that it was his glass one, she lacked the moral courage to do so.

In the hall scenes of horrible confusion were going forward; a perfect regiment of men tramped to and fro carrying things and bumping into each other. They all seemed furiously angry. Above the din could be heard the general's voice:

'What the——d'you think you're doing? Get out of that! Come here, blast you!'

Lady Prague, looking like a sort of boy scout,

61

was struggling with a strap when she caught sight of Jane.

'My dear girl,' she said taking one end of it from between her teeth, 'you can't come out in that mackintosh. Whoever heard of black on the hill? Why, it's no good at all. That scarlet cap will have to go too, I'm afraid. It's easy to see you haven't been up here before. We must alter all this.' She dived into a cupboard, and after some rummaging produced a filthy old Burberry and forced Jane to put it on. Evidently made for some portly man it hung in great folds on Jane and came nearly to her ankles.

'I don't think I'll take a mackintosh at all,' she said, rather peevishly, 'and I hardly ever wear a hat in any case, so I'll leave that behind, too.'

'As you like, my dear, of course. I think you'll be perished with cold and it will probably rain; it looks to me quite threatening. Have your own way, but don't blame me if—Hullo! we seem to be off at last.'

Jane climbed rather miserably into a sort of 'bus and sat next to Lady Prague. She was disappointed that Albert had not come, having taken particular pains with her appearance that morning on his account.

The moor was about five miles away, and during the whole drive nobody spoke a word except General Murgatroyd, who continually admonished his dog, a broken-looking retriever of the name of Mons.

'Lie down, will you? No, get off that coat!' (Kick, kick, kick; howl, howl, howl.) 'Stop that noise, blast you!' (Kick, howl.)

Jane pitied the poor animal which seemed unable

to do right in the eyes of its master.

When they arrived at their destination (a sort of sheep-track on the moor) they were met by two more guns who had come over from a neighbouring house to make up the numbers; and by a rabble of half-clothed and villainous-looking peasants armed for the most part with sticks. They reminded Jane of a film she had once seen called 'The Fourteenth of July.'

Their leader, an enormous man with red hair and wild eyes, came forward and addressed General Murgatroyd in a respectful but independent manner. When they had held a short parley he withdrew, and communicated the result of it to his followers, after which they all straggled away.

Jane supposed that they were the local unemployed, soliciting alms, and felt that the general must have treated them with some tact; once aroused, she thought, they might prove ugly customers.

Presently the whole party began to walk across the moor. Jane noticed that each of the men had an attendant who carried guns and a bag of cartridges. She wondered what their mission could be: perhaps to stand by and put the wounded birds out of their pain.

After an exhausting walk of about half an hour, during which Jane fell down several times (and the general said it would be easy walking, old humbug!), they arrived at a row of little roofless buildings, rather like native huts. The first one they came to was immediately, and silently, appropriated by Lord and Lady Prague, followed by their attendant.

Jane supposed that they were allocated in order

of rank and wondered which would fall to her lot.

'Better come with me, Miss Dacre,' said General Murgatroyd. It was the first time he had spoken except to swear at his dog, which he did continually, breaking the monotony by thrashing the poor brute, whose shrieks could be heard for miles across the heather.

When they reached his hut (or butt) he shouted in a voice of thunder:

'Get in, will you, and lie down.'

Jane, though rather taken aback, was about to comply when a kick from its master sent poor Mons flying into the butt, and she realized that the words had been addressed to that unfortunate and not to herself.

General Murgatroyd gave Jane his cartridge bag to sit on and paid no further attention to her. He and his attendant (the correct word for whom appeared to be *loader*) stood gazing over the top of the butt into space.

Seated on the floor, Jane could see nothing outside except a small piece of sky; she wondered why she had been made to leave her black mackintosh behind.

'I can neither see nor be seen. I expect it was that old woman's jealous spite. I don't believe she's a woman at all. She's just a very battered boy scout in disguise, and not much disguise, either.'

She began to suffer acutely from cold and cramp, and was filled with impotent rage. Eons of time passed over her. She pulled a stone out of the wall and scratched her name on another stone, then Albert's name, then a heart with an arrow through it (but she soon rubbed that off again). She knew the shape of the general's plus-fours and the pattern

64

of his stockings by heart, and could have drawn an accurate picture of the inside of the butt blindfold, when suddenly there was an explosion in her ears so tremendous that for an instant she thought she must have been killed. It was followed by several more in quick succession, and a perfect fusillade began, up and down the line. This lasted for about twenty minutes, and Jane rather enjoyed it—'As good as an Edgar Wallace play.'

At last it died away again, and General Murgatroyd said, 'Well, the drive's over. You can get up now, if you like.' Jane endeavoured to stand, but her legs would hardly carry her. After rubbing them for a bit she was just able to stagger out of the butt. She saw all around her the same band of peasants that had met them when they left the 'bus earlier that morning. Most of them were carrying dead grouse and picking up others.

'How kind!' she thought. 'The general has taken pity on the poor creatures and given them permission to gather the birds for their evening meal. He must really be nicer than he looks.'

Thinking of the evening meal made Jane realize that she was extremely hungry. 'Luncheon time soon, I expect.' She glanced at her watch. Only eleven o'clock! It must have stopped. Still ticking, though. Perhaps the hands had got stuck. She asked Admiral Wenceslaus the time.

'Nearly eleven, by Jove! We shall have to show a leg if we're to get in two more drives before lunch.'

Jane could hardly restrain her tears on hearing this. She sat hopelessly on a rock, while the rest of the party wandered about the heather looking for dead grouse.

When one of them found a bird he would whistle

65

up his dog and point to the little corpse saying, 'Seek hard,' and making peculiar noises in his throat. The dog would occasionally pick it up and give it into his master's hand, but more often would sniff away in another direction, in which case its master seized it by the scruff of the neck, rubbed its nose into the bird and gave it a good walloping.

Jane began to realize the full significance of the expression 'a dog's life.'

Lady Prague, who also strode about searching for grouse, presently came up to where Jane was sitting upon her rock, and asked why she didn't help.

'Because even if I did find a bird no bribe would induce me to touch it,' said Jane rather rudely, looking at Lady Prague's bloodstained hands.

In time the birds were all collected and hung upon the back of a small pony, and the party began to walk towards the butts from which the next drive was to take place. These were dimly visible on the side of the opposite mountain, and appeared to be a great distance away.

Jane walked by herself in a miserable silence, carefully watching her feet. In spite of this she fell down continually. The others were all talking and laughing over incidents of the drive. Jane admired them for keeping up their spirits in such circumstances. Their jokes were incomprehensible to her.

'I saw you take that bird of mine, old boy, but I wiped your eye twice, you know. Ha! Ha!'

'That dog o' yours has a good nose for other people's birds. Ha! Ha!'

'D'you remember poor old Monty at that very drive last year? All he shot was a beater and a bumble-bee.'

'Ah, yes! Poor Monty, poor Monty. Ha, ha, ha!'

The walk seemed endless. They came to a river which everyone seemed able to cross quite easily by jumping from stone to stone except Jane, who lost her balance in the middle and was obliged to wade. The water was ice-cold and came to her waist, but was not at first unpleasant, her feet were hot and sore, and both her ankles were swollen. Presently, however, the damp stockings began to rub her heels and every step became agony.

When they finally reached the butts Jane felt that she was in somewhat of a quandary. With whom ought she to sit this time? She hardly liked to inflict herself on General Murgatroyd again. Lord Prague and Captain Chadlington had their wives with them, and the admiral and Mr. Buggins were so very far ahead that she knew she would never have time to catch them up. She looked round rather helplessly, and saw standing near her one of the strangers who had come over for the day. As he was young and had a kind face, she ventured to ask if she might sit with him during the next drive. He seemed quite pleased and, making her a comfortable seat with his coat and cartridge bag, actually addressed her as if she were a human being. Jane felt really grateful; no one had so far spoken a word to her, except Lady Prague and General Murgatroyd, and they only from a too evident sense of duty.

The young man, whose name was Lord Alfred Sprott, asked if there was a cheery crowd at Dalloch Castle. Jane, more loyally than truthfully, said, 'Yes, a very cheery crowd.' She hoped that it was cheery where he was staying, too? He replied that it was top-hole, only a little stalking lodge, of course, but very cosy and jolly, quite a picnic. He told her some of the jolly jokes they had there. Jane, in her bemused condition, found him most entertaining; she laughed quite hysterically, and was sorry when the birds began to fly over them, putting an end to conversation.

In spite, however, of this spiritual sunshine Jane soon began to feel colder and more miserable even than before, and greatly looked forward to the next walk which might warm her up and dry her clothes.

This was not to be. While the birds were being picked up after that drive, she learnt, to her dismay, that the next one would take place from the same butts.

The wait between the two drives was interminable. Lord Alfred Sprott seemed to have come to the end of his witticisms and sat on his shooting-stick in a gloomy silence. Jane ventured one or two remarks, but they were not well received. She gathered that Lord Alfred had been shooting badly, and this had affected his spirits. She became more and more unhappy and shook all over with cold.

'I expect I shall be very ill after this,' she thought. 'I shall probably die, after lingering some weeks; then perhaps they will be sorry.' And tears of self-pity and boredom welled up in her eyes.

When the drive was over, they all began to walk towards the hut where luncheon was prepared. They were now obliged to keep in a straight line with each other, in order to put up game for the men, who carried their guns and let them off from time to time.

'Keep up please, Miss Dacre. Keep in line, please, or you'll be shot, you know.'

Jane thought that it seemed almost uncivilized to threaten an acquaintance that she must keep up or be shot, but she said nothing and struggled, fairly successfully, not to be left behind. As the result of this further misery one tiny bird was added to the bag.

CHAPTER EIGHT

Nothing in this world lasts for ever. The longest morning Jane could remember was at an end and the party had assembled in a little hut for luncheon. A good fire burnt in one corner and a smell of food and peat smoke created a friendly atmosphere. Jane felt happier, especially when she saw that Sally and Albert were seated on the floor in front of the fire.

Albert looked particularly alluring in an orange crêpe-de-chine shirt open at the neck, and a pair of orange-and-brown tartan trousers, tight to the knees and very baggy round the ankles. Under one arm he carried an old-fashioned telescope of black leather heavily mounted in brass, with which, he said, when asked why he had brought it, to view the quarry. He and Lord Alfred greeted each other with unconcealed disgust; they had been at Eton and Oxford together.

Luncheon was rather a silent meal. There was not nearly enough food to go round, and everyone was busy trying to take a little more than his or her share and then to eat it quickly for fear the others should notice. (The admiral choked rather badly from trying to save time by drinking with his mouth full. Lady Prague and General Murgatroyd thumped him on the back and made him look at the ceiling, after which he recovered.) Most of the baskets in which the food was packed seemed to contain a vast quantity of apples which nobody ate at all. Some very promising-looking packages were full of Petit-Beurre biscuits or dry bread, and the scarcity of food was rendered all the more tantalizing by the fact that what there was of it was quite excellent. The thermos flask which should have contained coffee proved to be empty.

Lady Prague and Lord Alfred carried on a desultory conversation about their mutual relations whose names appeared to be legion.

'I hear Buzzy has sold all his hunters.'

'Yes, I heard. An absolute tragedy, you know. But I'm afraid it's . . .'

'Yes, that's what my mother says. I don't know, though, really why it should be.'

'Well, my dear, every reason if you come to think of it. But what does Eileen say about all this—?'

'Haven't you heard?'

'No—what?'

'Eileen is staying down at Rose Dean.'

'No! Well, I must say I never, never would have thought it of her; though, mind you, I have always disliked Eileen. But really! Rose Dean—no that *is* a little too much. Then where is Looey? . . . (etc. etc.).' This was so interesting for everybody else.

When everything eatable had been consumed the general marshalled them all out of doors again. Admiral Wenceslaus was very indignant at this and said something to Jane about letting a cove finish his brandy in peace; but even he dared not mutiny and, muttering a few naval expressions, he followed the others out of the hut.

70

To Jane's great relief—for she was very tired and stiff—each of the women was now provided with a pony to ride. Albert walked between Jane's pony and Sally's. He looked round at the large crowd of people spread out over the moor, the ponies, dogs, and men with guns.

'We might be early settlers escaping from native tribes,' he observed. 'Led through unnatural hardships to civilization and safety by the iron will-power of one man, our beloved and sainted general. Alas, that within sight of help, his noble spirit should have flown. Poor, good old man, he will yet be enshrined in the heart of each one of us for ever.'

'Please don't laugh quite so loudly!' Lady Prague shouted to Jane and Sally, 'or all the birds will settle.'

'I wish,' said Albert, 'that I could spot an eagle or a stag with my telescope for the darling general to shoot at. He might take a fancy to me if I did. Our present lack of intimacy begins to weigh on my spirits.'

Albert searched the horizon with his telescope, but complained that, being unable to keep one eye shut, he saw nothing.

'If you ask me, I expect that's why the admiral rose from the ranks. Having only one eye, anyhow, he probably took prizes for viewing enemy craft quicker and more accurately than his shipmates. "A sail!—A sail! Ahoy!"' he cried, dancing a sort of hornpipe on the heather.

General Murgatroyd, who was beating his dog, stopped for a moment and asked Alfred Sprott if 'that fella thought the birds would be able to stand the sight of his orange shirt?' Lord Alfred grunted,

71

he could hardly stand the sight of it himself.

'I ducked him once,' he said, 'in Mercury.'

'Good boy! Did you, then? Good for you, sir!'

'This scenery,' said Albert to Jane, 'is really most amusing. It is curious how often natural scenery belongs to one particular era. The Apennines, for instance, are purely Renaissance: Savernake was made for the age of chivalry: Chantilly and Fontainebleau for the seventeenth and eighteenth centuries: the Rhine for the Middle Ages, and so on. At other times these landscapes seem beautiful, but unreal. Scotland, as you will no doubt have noticed, was invented by the Almighty for the delectation of Victoria and Albert. Foreseeing their existence, He arranged really suitable surroundings for them, and these purple mountains and mauve streams will stand as a reminder of the Victorian age long after the Albert Memorial has turned to dust.'

'What,' asked Jane, 'would you call the landscape of today?'

Albert did not answer, but said faintly:

'Aren't we nearly there; I'm most dreadfully tired?'

Sally jumped off her pony.

'Do ride instead of me for a bit, Albert; I wanted a walk.'

General Murgatroyd could hardly contain himself when he saw Albert, his graceful figure swaying slightly from the hips, seated upon Sally's pony. He was tired himself, though nothing would have induced him to say so; if Prague could still walk so could he. Lord Prague, it may be noted, was to all intents and purposes dead, except on shooting days when he would come to life in the most astonishing manner, walking and shooting with the best. At

72

other times he would sit in an arm-chair with his eyes shut and his hands folded, evidently keeping his strength for the next shoot. He hardly appeared able even to walk from his drawing-room to the dining-room and was always helped upstairs by his valet.

At about half a mile from their destination the horses were left behind and the party began to climb a fairly steep hill. When they reached the first butt Albert declared that he could go no farther and would stay where he was.

'That,' remarked Lord Alfred, who was passing it, 'is General Murgatroyd's butt.'

'Splendid!' And Albert, swinging himself on to the edge of it, sat there in a graceful position, his legs crossed, pretending to look through his telescope.

'Well, you'd better put on this mackintosh, Gates, that shirt would scare all the birds for miles.'

Lord Alfred went on his way feeling like the Good Samaritan.

Presently General Murgatroyd appeared with his loader. When he saw Albert he glared and muttered, but took no further notice of him and began to make his own arrangements for the drive.

'May I let off your gun, sir?' said Albert, pointing it straight into the general's face.

'Put that gun down this instant. My God! young man, I'm sure I don't know where you were brought up. When I was a kid I was sent to bed for a week because I pointed my toy pistol at the nurse.'

'I'm sorry,' said Albert, rather taken aback by his manner. 'I didn't know it was full.'

The general wiped his brow and looked round

73

helplessly.

'You can sit on that stone,' he said, indicating one at the bottom of the butt.

'Oh, sir, please, must I sit there? I wanted to watch you. I shan't see anything from down here. Oh, please, may I stand up?'

Receiving no answer beyond a frigid stare, Albert, with a deep sigh, disposed himself upon the stone, sitting cross-legged like an idol. He then produced a slim volume from his pocket. 'I presume that you have read "The Testament of Beauty," sir?'

'Never heard of it.'

'Oh, sir, you must have heard of it. A very great poem by our Poet Laureate.'

'No, I haven't; I expect it's immoral stuff, anyway. Kipling ought to be the Poet Laureate, to my mind.'

'Alas! Philistine that I am, I must disagree with you. I cannot appreciate Sir Rudyard's writings as no doubt I should. "Lest we forget, lest *we* forget,"' he chanted. 'Have you a favourite poem, sir?'

The general remained silent, his eye on the horizon. As a matter of fact he *had* a favourite poem, but could not quite remember how it went—

'Under the wide and starry sky
Dig my grave and let me lie.
Home is the hunter home from the hill,
And the hunter home from the hill.'

Something more or less like that.

'You care for T. S. Eliot, sir? But no, of course, I heard you cut off the wireless last night when Mrs.

74

Nicolson was about to read us some of his poems. How I wish I could be the one to convert you!' And he began to declaim in a loud and tragic voice:

'*We are the stuffed men, the hollow men* ...'

'Oh, *will* you be quiet? Can't you see the birds are settling?'

'I can see nothing from down here except the very *séant* pattern of your exquisite tweeds. But no matter.'

Albert read for a time in silence.

The general was breathing hard. Presently he stiffened:

'Over you!—over you, sir!' he shouted.

Albert dropped his book in a puddle and leapt to his feet, knocking the general's arm by mistake. The gun went off with a roar and a large number of birds flew over their heads unscathed.

'You blasted idiot! Why can't you sit still where I told you? Of all the damned fools I ever met—'

'I regret that I cannot stay here to be insulted,' said Albert; and he strolled out of the butt.

'Come back, will you? Blast you! Can't you see the bloody drive is beginning?'

Albert paid no attention, but walked gracefully away over the heather, telescope in hand, towards the next butt. Its occupant luckily happened to be Mr. Buggins, who was rather amused by and inclined to tolerate Albert, so there were no further *contretemps*. Meanwhile, the general, infuriated beyond control, was seen to fall upon his loader and shake him violently.

When this eventful drive was over, Jane, Sally and Albert, finding themselves close to a road where the motor-cars were waiting, took the heaven-sent opportunity to go home. Jane on her arrival went straight to bed, where she remained the whole of the following day, entertaining riotous parties in her bedroom. Her ankles were so swollen that it was nearly a week before she could walk without the aid of a stick.

CHAPTER NINE

Jane was enjoying herself passionately. Curiously enough, she thought, she had not fallen in love with Albert at all, but simply regarded him as a most perfect companion. Always cheerful and amusing, he was at the same time seriously intellectual and had the capacity of throwing himself heart and soul into whatever he happened to be doing. He and Jane had spent much of their time collecting together all the Victorian odds-and-ends that they could find in the house. These they assembled in the billiard-room, where Albert was now busy photographing them for a brochure which he intended to produce entitled 'Recent Finds at Dalloch Castle,' and which was to form a supplement to his larger work, 'Household Art of the Nineteenth Century.'

Jane, who had up till then maintained a wholesome superiority with regard to everything Victorian, quickly smothered this feeling, and learnt from Albert really to admire the bead stools, lacquer boxes, wax flowers and albums of water-colour sketches which so fascinated him.

They practically lived in the billiard-room, hard

at work the whole time, Albert making still-life compositions for his photographs, while Jane copied designs from chintzes and pieces of needlework in water-colours.

One day she was poking about in the attics trying to find more treasures for the catalogue when she noticed, poked away in a corner behind piles of furniture, a dusty glass dome. After a dangerous climb over rickety chests of drawers, derelict bedsteads and other rubbish, she managed to secure it and carry it to her bedroom, where she carefully removed the dome, which was opaque with dirt, expecting to discover some more wax fruit. Underneath it, however, she found to her amazement a representation in white wax of Jacob's Ladder. It was quite perfect. Jacob, in a sort of night-gown and an enormous beard, lay upon a floor of green plush. His head rested on a large square stone, and from just behind this rose the ladder, delicately balanced against wax clouds which billowed out of the green plush. Two angels were rather laboriously climbing on it (whether up or down it would be hard to say), while three more angels, supported by wires which rose from behind the clouds, hovered round about, twitching and quivering delightfully whenever the stand was moved.

Jane washed and replaced the dome, and then carried this treasure down to the billiard-room in great triumph. When Albert saw it his joy and delight knew no bounds.

'It is easily our most important find and shall be the frontispiece of my book!' he cried. 'I have never seen anything half so lovely. It is a poem! How can I find out the name of the artist? I must endeavour to do so without delay. But how sad, my dear, to think that this jewel should belong to people who so evidently have no feeling for beauty! It ought, of course, to occupy a place of honour in a museum. Never mind, I shall photograph it from every angle and in all lights, so that the artistic public will be able to gain some slight idea of its exquisite form, and thus share, to a certain extent, in my own emotions.'

At that moment Lady Prague was seen to pass by the open door, and Albert, longing to share his enthusiasm with somebody, rather thoughtlessly dashed out, seized her by the arm, and said:

'Lady Prague, do come and see our wonderful new find. Something to cause the greatest sensation among all cultured persons—so amusing, so exquisite, so stimulating...'

With the naïveté of a child showing off its new toy he led her up to the dome.

She stared at it for a moment, sniffed and said rather pityingly:

'What a lot of drip you do talk. Why, that's nothing more than a particularly unattractive form of dust-trap!'

She left the room.

All the excitement died out of Albert's face and was succeeded by an expression of the deepest disgust.

'Dust-trap!' he muttered between his teeth. 'You just wait until you see the booby-trap I'm going to make for you—you viviparous old vixen!'

Walter and Sally now came in and made up for Lady Prague's lack of appreciation by an enthusiasm almost as unbounded as Albert's. They walked round and round the dome, exclaiming:

'How beautiful!'—'How amusing!'—'That angel's so like Lord Prague, d'you see? And, of course, Jacob just *is* the admiral with a beard!'

'Green plush.
Admiral Jacob lay beneath a dome
Of crazy glass upon green plush.
And in this "nautical" posture
With angels rising from the Guinness foam
The Admiral
(Who was Jacob, too, out of the Bible)
Fell, bucolically, asleep.'

Even Lady Brenda was quite appreciative, saying that her children would simply love it.

'It reminds me so much of a lodging-house at Westgate where we used to go for our summer holidays when we were small. Every room in it had several domes of that sort.'

Albert breathlessly asked the address of this gold mine, but Lady Brenda had forgotten it and presently left them to go out fishing.

'What a disappointing woman that is,' said Jane when she had gone. 'I noticed her particularly in the train coming up here, and somehow thought she looked rather interesting. And then, when I heard her name, I was really excited to meet her. One's always being told how charming she is—so original and cultured. But she's a perfect fool, though I must say quite nice compared to old Prague.'

'She *is* cultured in the worst sort of way,' said Albert. 'But original! Oh, dear! I had a long conversation with her yesterday after tea so I know all about her originality. I'll tell you. She has, as I had supposed that she would, a green drawing-room with flower pictures which she picked up cheap (eighteenth century, so she says). She also has a stone-coloured dining-room with a sham stone floor. On the sideboard is a model of a ship. On the walls are old maps. The lights are shaded with maps. The firescreen is a map in needlework. The chairs are covered with *petit point* which she worked herself. Her bedroom is "very modern"; that is to say, it is painted silver and stippled all over. The ceiling is of Lalique glass as is the bed. The bathroom is painted to give the impression of a submarine forest. It has portholes instead of windows. I couldn't quite understand why.

'She reads few novels, but a great many "lives" and "memoirs." Her favourite novelists are Galsworthy, Masefield, David Garnett and Maurois, she "loves modern pictures, especially flower pictures," and admires some of John's portraits, but thinks Orpen the finest living artist. She has never been to the Tate Gallery, but always means to go.

'All this she told me herself, or rather I dug it out of her. I also gathered that she goes every year to the Ascot races in one of those picture-hats and a printed dress.'

'Four of them, you mean,' said Jane.

'Very likely. She goes quite often to the Embassy Night Club, but seldom stays up later than one or two o'clock. She has a great deal of committee work when in London, mostly connected with animals. Every year she goes for three weeks to Switzerland. Captain Chadlington prefers to stay at home and kill (foxes and birds), so she always goes with her great friend, Major Lagge, chaperoned by his sister and brother-in-law. Those sort of women, I have so often noticed, never take lovers, but they have some great friend with whom they go about literally like brother and sister. It is all most peculiar and unhealthy. I think, myself, that she is a creature so overbred that there is no sex or brain left, only nerves and the herd instinct. There are many like that in English society, a sufficiently uninteresting species. I find her, in a way, beautiful.'

'Oh, yes, she is certainly that,' said Jane, 'although personally, I can't admire her very much. She has such a maddening expression. And she's really very nice, too, you know. She's been sweet to Sally and me.'

'And her husband is good-looking. But what a dreary personality he has, most uncompanionable. I suppose he will in time become a sort of Murgatroyd, although I doubt whether he will ever acquire that *joie de vivre* which so characterizes the dear general.'

'Beastly old man!'

'Ah, no, Jane! I must admit to a very great *penchant* for the general. He is so delightfully uncompromising. Yesterday I heard him say that before the War the things he hated most were Roman Catholics and Negroes, but now, he said, banging on the table, now it's Germans. I wonder what he would do if he met a Roman Catholic Negro with a German father! Dare I dress up as one and see? I could black my face, wear a rosary and Prussian boots and come in crossing myself and singing "The Watch on the Rhine" to the tune of a Negro spiritual.'

Jane laughed.

'I'm afraid you must think me rather idiotic, my

81

dear Jane. I have been in such spirits since I came up here. I can assure you that I am quite a different person in Paris—all hard work and no play, or very little. But, after all, it is the "hols." here, as we used to say, and talking of "hols.," do help me to think out a good practical joke for Lady Prague. How I hate that old woman! Do you think she and the general—Ah! General! What a delightful surprise! I imagined that you were busy stalking those grouse again.'

'No, Gates, we are not. Very few moors can be shot over more than four times a week, you know.'

'That *must* be a relief,' said Albert sympathetically.

The general looked with some disapproval at his *matelot* clothes—a pair of baggy blue trousers worn with a blue-and-white sweater and a scarlet belt, and said severely:

'If you will be so good as to clear that mess off the table, we were going to play billiards.'

'Oh, sir, this is dreadful! You could not possibly play on the floor, I suppose? No? Well, if you'll most kindly wait for one moment while I photograph this exquisite object which Jane has found, I shall be really grateful.'

Captain Chadlington and Admiral Wenceslaus now came in. The admiral was airing his favourite topic, Blockade.

'Oh, it was a terrible scandal. Thirty thousand tons of toffee found their way through Holland alone, my dear Chadlington, and this is a most conservative estimate, worked out by my friend Jinks (whose book on the subject I have lent to your wife). Many of the Germans taken prisoner at that time by our chaps had their pockets bulging with

82

British toffee. British toffee, my dear Chadlington!

'And then,' he added, with a catch in his voice, 'the glycerine!'

'Were their pockets bulging with that, too?' asked Captain Chadlington, who, as a prospective candidate for Parliament, was always ready to learn.

'Not their pockets. Dear me, no! Far, far worse than that—their shell-cases!'

'Oh, I say! That's disgraceful!'

'It is! Monstrous! But what I want to know is—who was the traitor? Read Page on the subject. He couldn't understand it—not a word. He couldn't make out what we were driving at. Why don't they blockade?—What on earth are you doing, Gates?'

Albert, balanced gracefully on a step-ladder, was taking a photograph of the Jacob's Ladder as seen from above.

'There,' he said, 'that's done. Now I will clear the table and you can play your little game.'

CHAPTER TEN

Jane and Albert did not stay to watch the billiards but strolled into the garden.

'I saw them playing yesterday evening,' said Albert. 'It is a curious but not a graceful game, and terribly monotonous. If it weren't such a beautiful day I should have advised you to watch them for a little, all the same: it is always interesting to see how others find their recreation. They play with ivory balls and long, tapering sticks.'

'Yes, I know,' said Jane. 'Look! there's Mr.

Buggins sketching.'

'How delightful. We must go and talk to him.'

Mr. Buggins was sketching the old part of the house in water-colours; that is to say, he had drawn it with a pencil and was now busy colouring it in with small, rather dry brushes. It was careful work.

When he saw Albert approaching he was very much embarrassed, knowing quite well the attitude of the professional artist to the painstaking amateur; so, to cover his own confusion and to save Albert from feeling obliged to make a polite criticism of his work, he began to talk very fast about the house and its history.

'I love this part of the house, you know. That tower, and of course, the dungeons, were all that escaped the Great Fire in 1850. It is immensely old, probably eleventh century, and the walls are so thick that Lady Craigdalloch has been able to put two water-closets in the thickness alone.'

'How jolly for her!' said Albert, feeling that some remark was called for.

'Yes, very. Of course you know the history attaching to that tower?'

'No; do tell us, Mr. Buggins. I was thinking that there must be some legends connected with the castle.'

Jane and Albert sat down on the grass, and Mr. Buggins, clearing his throat, began his story.

'One of the Thanes of Dalloch,' he said, 'as they were then called, had a very beautiful daughter, the Lady Muscatel. Her apartment was in that tower, where she would sit all day spinning. At night, when the moon was full, she would often lean out of her window and gaze at it, and one night she was doing so when she heard from beneath her a faint

84

noise of singing. Looking down, she beheld the handsome features of a young man of high degree, who told her that he had lost his way while out hunting.

'"Alas!" she said, "my father and brothers are from home, and I dare not open to you in their absence."

'He told her that he would not dream of trespassing on her hospitality and retired, fortified by a bottle of wine which she lowered to him in a basket.

'The next night he came again, and the next, and soon they were passionately in love with each other. But little did the unfortunate Muscatel realize that her lover was the only son of Thane McBane, head of a clan which her father was even then planning to exterminate. The warlike preparations for this raid which were going forward in the castle left the Lady Muscatel more and more to her own devices, so that one day she was able to leave her tower and go with Ronnie McBane to the nearest priest, who married them. Even so they dared not fly, but thought it better to wait until they should hear of a ship bound for France. Poor children! They knew full well that both their fathers would see them dead sooner than married (for Ronnie had by now divulged his fearful secret).

'At last Dalloch's preparations were completed and he and his men sallied forth, armed to the teeth, to wipe out the McBanes. The battle was a fearful one, but the conclusion was foregone. The unfortunate McBanes, taken unawares and overwhelmed by numbers, fought with the courage of desperation. One by one they fell, but each one that died accounted for three or four of the

85

Dallochs. Ronnie McBane was the last to succumb, and when he did so, bleeding from forty desperate wounds, it was with the knowledge that no fewer than thirty-two of his enemies, slain by his own hand, had preceded him. It was one of the bloodiest fights in the history of the clans.

'That evening the Lady Muscatel heard sounds of merry-making in the great hall, where her father and the wild clansmen were celebrating their victory with wine and song. She went down to see what was happening and the first thing that met her eyes was Ronnie's head, horribly mutilated, on a pike. The shock proved too much for her reason and she soon became insane, wandering about the house and crying for her lost love. When her child was born neither she nor it survived many days.

'They say that at the full moon she can still be heard, wailing, wailing; and some even declare that they have seen her wan form, carrying the head of her lover.

'But surely you have heard the *Lament of the Lady Muscatel*? No? It is a beautiful ballad. Personally, I think it one of the most beautiful that Scotland has produced, although it is comparatively little known. Let me see if I can remember it.' And clearing his throat, he recited the following ballad:

THE LAMENT OF THE LADY MUSCATEL

*My lo'e he war winsome, my lo'e he war braw
    [Brave],
Every nicht 'neath my windie he cam'.
He wad sing, oh, sae saft, till the nicht it waur
    o'er
I' the morn he was sadly gang ham'.*

The pibroch i' the glen is bonny,
But waley, waley, wheer's ma Ronnie?

His e'en they were blew and his mou [Mouth] *it*
  war red,
And his philabeg [Kilt] *cam' to the knee;*
But noo ma puir Ronnie he's skaithless and deid,
Ah, wud that I a'so could dee.

The pibroch i' the glen is bonny,
But waley, waley, wheer's ma Ronnie?

I ganged ma gait sairly to yon branksome brae,
Wheer ma true loe war killed i' the ficht,
I sat on a creepy [Little stool] *and I greeted*
  [Cried, bewailed] *the day,*
And I sat greeting there till the nicht.

The pibroch i' the glen is bonny,
But waley, waley, wheer's ma Ronnie?

Ah, Ronnie, my true lo'e ah, Ronnie, mine ane,
Shall I niver muir see ye ava?
I see your life's bluid poured out o'er yonder
  stane,
But your sperrit has flane far awa.

The pibroch i' the glen is bonny,
But waley, waley, wheer's ma Ronnie?

They gave me your heid, Ronnie, wropped oop i'
  sae [Silk] *,*

87

And I buried it 'neath yonder saugh [Willow
    tree];
For ye've left me, my Ronnie, to gang a' agley
And I niver shall see ye nae muir.

    The pibroch i' the glen is bonny,
    But waley, waley, wheer's ma Ronnie?

Ma mither she mad' me ane parritch o' kail,
And she gave me ane snood for ma heid;
But a' I can do is to greet and to wail,
Ah, Mither, I wud I were deid.

    The pibroch i' the glen is bonny,
    But waley, waley, wheer's ma Ronnie?

But e'er the sun rise, Mither, muir o'er the brae,
And e'er ane muir morrow shall dawn;
My heid on its pillow sae saftly I'll lay,
But ma sperrit to him will ha' flawn.

    The pibroch i' the glen is bonny.
    But waley, waley, wheer's ma Ronnie?

There was a short silence, broken by Albert, who said: 'How beautiful, and what a touching story! We must tell it to Walter; he will be so much interested and might, I feel, write one of his charming poems round it. I think the ballad quite the finest I have ever heard.'

'I think so, too,' said Mr. Buggins, who had rarely known such an appreciative audience and was greatly enjoying himself. 'To the student of mediaeval Scottish history it is, of course, extremely illuminating, being so full of allusions to old

88

customs, many of which survived until quite recently.'

'Were there many allusions of that sort?' asked Albert. 'They escaped me.'

'Yes, of course, because you are not conversant with the history of those times. But take, for instance, the line: "And his philabeg cam' to the knee." This is very significant when you know, as I do, that only three clans in all Scotland wore their philabeg to the knee—that is, covering the knee: the McBanes, the Duffs of Ogle and the McFeas. Their reasons for doing so open up many aspects of clan history. The McBanes wore it to the knee in memory of Thane Angus McBane, who, when hiding from the English soldiery in some bracken was given away by the shine of his knees; his subsequent brutal treatment and shameful death will, of course, be well known to you.'

'Of course,' murmured Albert, not wishing to appear too ignorant. 'This is all so fascinating,' he added. 'Why did the other two tribes wear it to the knee?'

'The Duffs of Ogle because they used a very curious type of long bow which could only be drawn kneeling. (You will often have heard the expression: "To Duff down," meaning "to kneel.") This gave great numbers of them a sort of housemaid's knee, so one of the Thanes gave an order that their philabegs must be made long enough for them to kneel on. The McFeas, of course, have always worn it very long on account of the old saw:

"Should McFea show the knee,
The Devil's curse upon him be."

89

Am I boring you?'

'On the contrary,' said Albert, 'I am very deeply interested. I have so often wondered what the origin of "to Duff down" could be and now I know. Do tell us some more.'

'You may remember,' continued Mr. Buggins, 'that one verse of the Lady Muscatel's ballad begins:

'"*They gave me your heid, Ronnie, wropped oop i' sae.*"

'This, of course, sounds rather peculiar—*sae*, you know, is *silk*—until you remember that only a man who had killed with his own hand in fair battle over forty warriors was entitled to have "his heid wropped oop i' sae" after his death. It was an honour that was very eagerly sought by all the clansmen and it must have consoled the Lady Muscatel in her great sorrow that she was able "to wrop her beloved's heid oop i' sae." There is a very curious legend connected with this custom.

'A young laird of Tomintoul died, they say of poison, in his bed, having only killed in his lifetime some thirty-nine warriors. His widow was distracted with grief and, although about to become a mother, she cut off his right hand, clasped it round a dirk and went herself into the thick of the fight. When she had slain one man with her husband's hand, she was able to go home and "wrop his heid oop i' sae." The Tomintouls to this day have as their family crest a severed hand with a dirk in memory of Brave Meg, as she was called. Those were strangely savage days, I often think.'

'Tell us some more,' said Jane.

'Let me see: what else can I remember? Oh, yes. The Lady Muscatel goes on to say: "I buried him 'neath yonder saugh." Up to comparatively recent times any man who had been killed by his father-in-law's clansmen was buried beneath a *saugh* (willow tree). There are some parts of Scotland where it would be impossible to find a saugh for miles that had not a grassy mound before it, telling a bloody tale. Tradition says that Ronnie's body was later exhumed and laid beside those of his wife and child in the chapel. "I sat on a creepy." A creepy was a wooden stool, often three-legged, on which women would sit to greet (or bewail) the loss of a loved one killed in the fight.'

'But was the fight always going on?' asked Albert.

'Very, very constantly. The wild clansmen were generally engaged in deadly feuds, which were often continued over many generations and were treated almost as a religion.'

'What,' asked Jane, 'is a "parritch o' kail"?'

'I am glad you mentioned that. *A parritch o' kail* is a curious and very intoxicating drink made of cabbage and oatmeal. Perhaps her mother hoped that the Lady Muscatel would drown her sorrows in it. Dear me!' he said, gathering up his painting materials, 'how I must have bored you.'

'My dear sir,' cried Albert, '*tout au contraire!* I'm entranced. But tell us one thing before you go. Have you ever seen the Lady Muscatel's ghost?'

'Alas! I have not; but Craigdalloch says that as a child he saw her constantly, sometimes looking out of the window' (he pointed to a little window in the tower)—'but more often walking in the great corridor which leads to her apartment. He has told me that she wears a grey wimple snood (you remember that she refers to a *snood* in the ballad),

91

and carries in one hand a sort of parcel—the "heid," no doubt, "wropped oop i' sae." She is supposed to walk when the moon is full.'

The rasping voice of Lady Prague suddenly broke in upon them, causing Albert and Mr. Buggins to leap to their feet.

'Who is supposed to walk when the moon is full?'

Mr. Buggins told her the story rather shortly.

'Well,' she said, 'and I suppose you believe that sort of balderdash. Tosh—bosh and nonsense! Personally, I shall believe in ghosts when I have seen one, and not before. Surely you must have noticed by now that everyone knows somebody else who has seen a ghost, but they've never seen one themselves.'

'But Craig has seen the Lady Muscatel.'

'Craig! Silly old man, he'd see anything. I expect it was really a housemaid, if you ask me.'

She blew her nose and went towards the castle.

'Such a golden nature,' said Albert pensively. 'One would hardly credit her with second sight, but still one never knows: the most unlikely people see ghosts—sometimes.'

★   ★   ★

That night Lady Prague took her bath, as she always did, before going to bed. She lay in the water for some time without washing very much; then dried herself briskly and put on a linen night-dress trimmed with crochet-lace, a pair of quilted slippers and a Chinese kimono with storks and fir-trees embroidered all over it. Thus attired, with her hair screwed in to a small lump on the top of her head, and a towel and a pair of combinations

92

over one arm, she sallied forth into the great corridor. As she did so she noticed that the lights, by some mistake, had all been put out; but she was easily able to see her way because a curtain at the other end of the corridor was drawn back and a great shaft of moonlight fell through the window on to the carpet.

Lady Prague shuffled along until she had nearly reached her bedroom door, when suddenly she stood still, rooted to the ground with terror. A female form, immensely tall and unnatural-looking, had stepped into the shaft of moonlight. In its hand was a sort of round parcel which it held out towards the paralysed peeress; then, emitting a soft but terrifying wail, it vanished into the shadows. The sound of this wail seemed to unloosen Lady Prague's own tongue, and shriek upon piercing shriek resounded through the house.

Bedroom doors on every side now flew open and startled guests rushed out to the assistance of the fainting baroness. Albert, one of the first to be on the spot, quickly helped the poor lady to a chair, where she sat and rocked herself to and fro, moaning and sobbing in a distracted manner.

'What is the matter, Lady Prague?' said Albert sharply. 'Come, come now, you must try and pull yourself together: you are hysterical, you know. What is it? Are you ill?'

'Oh, oh! oh!' said Lady Prague in a sort of moaning sing-song. 'I saw her! I saw her! I saw her!'

'Whom did you see?'

'Oh! oh! oh! I saw her! ... Lady Muscatel! She was over by that window ... Oh! oh! oh!'

'Fetch some water, Jane dear, will you?' said

Albert. 'Now, Lady Prague, you are quite safe, you know, with us.'

'Let her talk about it,' said Mr. Buggins in an undertone, 'it will do her good. How I envy you, Lady Prague: it has been the dream of my life to see someone from another world and, of all people, Muscatel. How did she look?'

'Oh! oh! oh! ... Dreadful! ... All in grey, with a wimple snood ...'

'Nonsense!' said Albert, but nobody heard him.

'And she was holding a sort of parcel ... Oh! oh! oh!'

'The heid, no doubt, "wropped oop i' sae." *How* I do envy you! She didn't speak, I suppose?'

'Oh! oh! oh! ... Yes, she did. She did: "Ronnie! Ronnie! mine ane Ronnie!"'

'Oh, you old liar!' said Albert, under his breath.

Jane, on her way back with a glass of water, nearly tripped up over something outside Albert's bedroom. It proved on investigation to be a large bath sponge wrapped up in a silk handkerchief. Suspicions that she had already entertained as to the true identity of the Lady Muscatel now crystallized into certainty. She put the sponge into Albert's bed; then, controlling her laughter, she rejoined the others and gave the water to Lady Prague, who drank it gratefully. She appeared to be partially restored and was describing her experience in some detail, looking searchingly at Albert as she did so.

'The worst part,' she said, 'of the whole thing was the creature's face, which I saw quite plainly in the moonlight. It was not so much mad as foolish and idiotic. Really, I assure you, the stupidest face I ever saw.'

'She has guessed,' thought Jane.

94

'Come, Lady Prague,' said Albert, 'not as bad as all that surely; not idiotic?'

'Perhaps *wanting*, more than idiotic, and hideous beyond belief.'

Later, when they were all returning to their rooms and peace had descended upon the house, Jane said to Albert:

'You know, my dear, she scored in the end.'

'I'm afraid,' he replied, 'that she did.'

CHAPTER ELEVEN

'Suddenly, just in time, I realized that he was a filthy Hun, so of course I turned my back on him and refused to shake hands. I think he noticed; anyway, I hope so. I hope he felt his position.'

General Murgatroyd looked round triumphantly. It was the end of dinner. The women had left the dining-room, and the general who had been shooting that day with the son of an old friend who had taken a neighbouring moor, was telling his experiences.

'Quite right, Murgatroyd. That's the way to treat 'em—the swine! Now, if only we had blockaded them from the very first he wouldn't have been alive to-day, with any luck.'

The admiral swilled off his seventh glass of port.

'Never shake hands with niggers, Catholics or Germans if I can help it,' continued the general.

Walter, knowing that Albert was an ardent pacifist and foreseeing some trouble, tried to change the conversation by asking him how his work had progressed that day; but the latter, whose face was

95

burning, took no notice of him. Leaning towards General Murgatroyd he said in a level voice:

'Is this the way you always behave when you meet an ex-enemy, even under the roof of a mutual friend?'

'Of course—the filthy swine!' shouted the general. 'And so would you, young man, if you'd been through the last war. I think it's the most shocking thing—the way some of you young people have quite forgotten what your elders suffered in those four years.'

'We haven't exactly forgotten it,' said Albert; 'but it was never anything to do with us. It was your war and I hope you enjoyed it, that's all,' he added, losing all control over himself. 'You made it, as you are trying, by disgusting rudeness to citizens of a great and friendly nation, to make another one, trying your very hardest, too, on your own admission. But let me tell you that even when you have succeeded, even when you have brought another war upon us, it won't be any good. None of my generation will go and fight. We don't care for wars, you see. We have other things to think about.'

'Albert, *please*!' said Walter, 'don't let's talk about this any more,' he begged; but no one paid any attention to him.

Great veins stood out on the general's forehead.

'Do you mean that you would sit still and do nothing to prevent your country being invaded, governed, by a lot of filthy foreigners?'

'Really, General, I cannot feel that it would necessarily harm the country. Many of us hope in time to see, under one government, the United States of Europe, which was Napoleon's dream.

96

The Germans are a people of undoubted culture and known for their exceptional efficiency. I daresay we should be no worse off under their administration than we are at present. If it is on sentimental grounds that you object to it, remember that for over a hundred years of undoubted prosperity England was ruled over by German—even German-speaking sovereigns.'

The general tried to speak, but Albert continued ruthlessly:

'People of your class notoriously enjoy wars and fighting. This is only natural. You have been educated to that end. Your very recreations consist entirely in killing things, and it is clearly more exciting to kill men than rabbits or foxes. But in future you will do well to avoid stirring up the great civilized nations against each other. That's all.'

'Quite right,' said Lord Prague, who imagined from the few words that had penetrated to his consciousness and from Albert's impassioned manner that he was reviling all foreigners. 'That is the proper spirit, Mr. Gates. Down with the Huns! Down with the Frogs! Down with the Macaronis! Down with Uncle Sam! England for the English!'

Exhausted by the effort of this oration he lay back once more in his chair and closed his eyes.

Nobody paid any attention to him, and there was a long silence, accentuated by heavy breathing and the sound of the admiral gulping down his thirteenth glass of port.

At last it was broken by Mr. Buggins.

'Gates is, of course, entitled to his own opinions. I can see his point of view although, naturally, it differs from my own. Being very young and very enthusiastic, he expresses himself violently and rashly and probably says a great deal more than he means. None the less, there is something to be said for his argument.

'All cultured persons are, to a certain extent, cosmopolitan. They feel at home among people of equal culture to whatever nationality they may happen to belong. I feel this very strongly myself. Italy is to me a second Fatherland; although I have no Italian blood I feel as much at home there as I do in England, having perhaps more congenial friends in Rome than I have anywhere else.

'Gates, who is an artist—may I remind you?—of recognized ability, would feel naturally more at his ease among other artists, whatever their nationality, than he would, say, in the company of English foxhunting squires.

'Artists, poets, musicians and writers are, of course, less affected by the governments under whose rule they may happen to find themselves than perhaps any other class. Therefore, it is hardly surprising if they do not greatly mind what form that government takes—'

'Then are loyalty and patriotism to count for nothing?' the general interrupted in a furious voice.

'Nothing at all!' said Lord Prague, who had opened his eyes again and appeared anxious to take part in the argument.

'Patriotism,' said Albert, 'is a virtue which I have never understood. That it should exist in any but the most primitive minds has always mystified me. I regard it as one step higher than the Chinese family worship, but it seems to me that at our stage of civilization we should have got past all that sort of thing.

'I am very glad, certainly, to be English-speaking. That I regard as a very great advantage, both as a matter of convenience and also because there is no language so rich in literature. Otherwise, what is there to be proud of in this hideous island, where architecture generally vies with scenery to offend the eye and which has produced no truly great men, none to compare with, for instance, Napoleon?'

'I should have thought, my dear Gates, if I may say so, that with your strongly pacifist views you would look upon Napoleon as the most despicable of men,' said Mr. Buggins.

'No, indeed; Napoleon was the greatest of all pacifists. He fought only for peace, and would have achieved what I spoke of just now—the United States of Europe, except for the jealous and pettifogging policy of certain British statesmen.'

'That, I should say, is a matter of opinion, and I doubt whether you are right,' said Mr. Buggins. 'But at the same time, Gates, there is something I should like to say to you, which is, that I think you have no right to speak as you did of the men who fought in the War, sneering at them and hoping they enjoyed it, and so on. I know you did not really mean to say much, but remember that sort of thing does no good and only creates more bitterness between our two generations, as though enough did not exist already. I know that many of us seem to you narrow-minded, stupid and unproductive. But if you would look a little bit below the surface you might realize that there is a reason for this. Some of us spent four of what should have been our best years in the trenches.

'At the risk of boring I will put my own case before you.

'When the War broke out I was twenty-eight. I had adopted literature as my profession and was at that time art critic on several newspapers. I had also written and published two books involving a great deal of hard work and serious research—the first, a life of Don John of Austria, the second, an exhaustive treatise on the life and work of Cervantes. Both were well received and, encouraged by this, I was, in 1914, engaged upon an extensive history of Spain in the time of Philip II, dealing in some detail with, for instance, the art of Velasquez and El Greco, the events which led to the battle of Lepanto, the religious struggle in the Netherlands, and so on. I had been working hard at this for three years and had collected most of my material.

'On the 5th August, 1914, whether rightly or wrongly, but true to the tradition in which I had been brought up, I enlisted in the army. Later in that year I received a commission. I will not enlarge upon the ensuing years, but I can't say that I found them very enjoyable.

'When, in 1919, I was demobilized, I found that, as far as my work was concerned, my life was over—at the age of thirty-three. I was well off financially. I had leisure at my disposal. I had my copious notes. Perhaps—no doubt, in fact—it was a question of nerves. Whatever the reason, I can assure you that I was truly incapable of such concentrated hard work as that book would have required. I had lost interest in my subject and faith in myself. The result is that I am now an oldish man, of certain culture, I hope, but unproductive, an amateur and a dilettante. I know it. I despise myself for it, but I cannot help it.

'And that, I am convinced, is more or less the

story of hundreds of my contemporaries.

'Everybody knows—you are at no pains to conceal it—that the young people of to-day despise and dislike the men and women of my age. I suppose that never since the world began have two generations been so much at variance. You think us superficial, narrow-minded, tasteless and sterile, and you are right. But who knows what we might have become if things had been different?

'That is why I do earnestly beg of you not to speak sarcastically, as you did just now, of the men who fought in the War. Leave us, at any rate, the illusion that we were right to do so.'

'Oh dear!' said Albert. 'How you do misunderstand me! I suppose I must express myself very badly. Of course I feel the greatest respect and admiration for the men who fought. I am only criticizing those unprincipled members of the governing classes (of all nationalities) who made it necessary for them to do so—men to whose interest it is that there should be wars. Professional soldiers, for instance, must naturally wish for war or all their work and training of years would be for nothing. Many politicians find in it a wonderful opportunity for self-aggrandizement. Certain business men make vast fortunes out of it. These are the people who are responsible. They educate the young to believe that war is right so that when they have manufactured it they are supported by all classes.

'But they ought to be regarded with the deepest distrust by their fellow citizens, instead of which they are set up as national heroes. I would have their statues removed from all public places and put where they belong—in the Chamber of

101

Horrors—thus serving the cause both of Art and of Morals.'

He glared at the general, who returned his black looks with interest, but could not trust himself to speak.

'General Murgatroyd,' continued Albert, 'provoked this discussion by actually boasting (though I don't know how he can dare even to admit such a thing) that he is doing his best in every way to make another war. Not content with rising in his bloody profession over the dead bodies of hundreds of innocent men, he evidently continues to be a propagandist of the most insidious and dangerous type. Happily, however, mankind is beginning to realize that war is of all crimes the most degraded; and when, which will soon happen, the great majority holds that view, peace will be permanent and universal. Generals, on that rapidly approaching day, will become as extinct as the dodo, relegated to the farcical side of drama and the films.'

'Come!' exclaimed Mr. Buggins, feeling that enough had now been said, 'come, Mowbray, and have a game of billiards.'

But the general, deeply incensed, retired to the study, where he listened to *Iolanthe* on the wireless and read his favourite book, *Tegetmeer on Pheasants*.

Admiral Wenceslaus, having finished the port, tottered off to bed, eye in hand, singing, 'The more we are together.'

CHAPTER TWELVE

After this rather acrimonious dinner, Albert, noticing that there was a very lovely full moon and that the air outside was warm and mellow, suggested to Jane that they should go out for a little walk. She thought that it would be a good idea. The evenings at Dalloch were apt to be rather boring. Lady Prague had introduced a particularly odious form of paper game, called briefly and appropriately 'Lists,' which consisted of seeing who could make the longest list of boys' names, fishes, kinds of material, diseases and such things beginning with a certain letter. As Lady Prague herself always chose both the subject and the letter, and as she invariably won, it was felt, no doubt unjustly, that she sat up for hours every night with a dictionary preparing herself for the next game. The only time they had played anything else it had been at Albert's suggestion—Consequences, but this was not an unqualified success.

For the erotic Lady Prague to meet the sobered-up Admiral Wenceslaus in a bedroom, undressing; for her to say to him, 'What about it?'; for him to say to her, 'My eye!'; for the consequence to be that they had nine children in three lots of triplets; and for the world to say, 'The only compensation for regurgitation is re-assimilation,' had been considered too embarrassing to risk repetition. (Albert, accused afterwards of cheating, had hotly denied the charge.)

'I couldn't have faced "Lists" again,' said Jane as they walked away from the castle. 'Somehow I seem

103

to get worse and worse at it. Last night, for instance, I couldn't even think of one vegetable beginning with "c", of course—*cabbage*. It was too idiotic; all I could think of was brussels sprouts and broccoli; and I knew they were wrong.'

'Yes; indeed; it is ghastly. The diseases are the most embarrassing, though.'

'And the vices. I think it's a horrid game.'

Albert told her of the conversation that had just taken place in the dining-room and asked what her feelings were on the subject.

'Oh! the same as yours! All young people must surely agree about that except, I suppose, young soldiers, but I don't count them anyway.'

Jane had once been in love for a short time with an officer in the Guards and had looked upon the army with a jaundiced eye ever since. (She had treated him abominably.)

'Mr. Buggins agrees with us, too. Of course, he had to qualify his approval with the general listening like that, but I could see exactly what he really meant. I think him so charming; at first he seemed a little tiresome with all his culture and folk-lore and good taste, but now I'm becoming very fond of him. He told us a lot about himself after dinner, but never mentioned anything about his wife. I wonder when all that happened?'

'Poor man! He looks dreadfully sad, I always think. He's the only nice one among the grown-ups here, isn't he?'

'Yes, indeed he is. I don't know what would have happened this evening if he hadn't been there. I should probably have insulted General Murgatroyd even more than I did, and then have been obliged to leave the house, the very last thing I wish to do at the moment.'

Jane suddenly began to feel embarrassed. It had come upon her lately with a certainty born of experience that Albert was falling in love with her, and now she began to think from the absent-minded way in which he spoke and his general manner that he was about to make some sort of declaration. This was the very last thing Jane wanted to happen.

She had been considering the situation and had decided that although she liked Albert more than anybody she had ever met, and although she would probably marry him in the end, she was not at present in love with him. On the other hand she did not at all want to lose him entirely, which might happen if he proposed and was refused. She was anxious for things to go on as they were at present. So she kept up a sort of barrage of rather foolish, nervous chatter.

'Do you know,' said Albert interrupting her in the middle of a sentence, and standing still, 'that I'm in love with you, Jane?'

Her heart sank.

'Are you, Albert?' she said faintly, wondering what the next move would be.

There was a silence. Albert, taking her hand, kissed her fingers one by one.

'Well?'

Jane said nothing. He took her in his arms and began kissing her face.

'Do you love me, darling?'

Jane felt frightened suddenly of committing herself to anything and said in an unnatural way:

'Albert, I don't know—I'm not sure.'

He let go of her at once, saying rather coldly:

'No, I see. Well, if you change your mind you'd better tell me, will you? Let's go on walking, it's such a lovely night.'

She thought this would be almost too embarrassing, but soon felt curiously at her ease, as though nothing had happened at all. They were in a wood of little fir trees which reminded her of a German fairy story she had been fond of as a child. She told it to Albert as they walked along. Presently, they came out of the wood on to the open moor. The moon, which was enormous, shone in a perfectly empty sky; the moor looked like the sea. There was a very complete silence.

As they stood there for a moment before turning back, Jane suddenly realized with a wave of feeling how much she loved Albert. She passionately hoped now that he would take her in his arms and kiss her, but he did not do so and a strange feeling of shyness prevented her from making an opening for him.

After standing there for some time in silence they returned to the castle, talking quite naturally about everyday things. They found that all the others had gone to bed, and crept up the back stairs in complete darkness, saying good night affectionately when they reached their bedrooms.

*   *   *

Jane lay awake for hours that night, tingling all over with excitement and trying to concentrate on the foregoing events with some degree of calmness.

'He never said anything about marriage,' she thought. 'Probably he has no intention of marrying me: artists seldom want the extra responsibility of a wife. And then he probably has very modern ideas on the subject. No, he evidently means it to be just an *affaire*. Anyhow, to-morrow I shall tell him that I love him. Then, if he wants me to be his mistress, we can run away to Paris together when we leave here, but not before. I can't have Sally involved.'

Jane was delighted with this idea. Marriage had always seemed to her rather a dull and pompous business, but to run away to Paris as the mistress of a handsome young artist would be the height of romance, and would probably scandalize her parents and relations. (Jane's one mission in life seemed to be to alienate her family, of whom she was, if she had only realized it, extremely fond, and nobody would have been more upset or annoyed than she herself if she had succeeded.)

As she lay watching the flickering firelight she suddenly had a mental vision of Albert's good-looking face as it had appeared when he said, 'Do you love me, darling?'

'Yes! yes! yes! Albert, sweetest, I do! And I'll tell you so tomorrow.'

And Jane fell rapturously asleep.

She was awakened at a very early hour by the sound of furious voices in the hall. She knew that this indicated the departure of the shooters (or guns) for another happy day on the moors.

'But why "guns",' she thought sleepily. 'After all, one doesn't speak of people as "paint brushes" or "pens". And why does it always make them cross when they are supposed to enjoy it so enormously? Of course, they simply loathe it really, poor things, and no wonder.'

General Murgatroyd and Lady Prague came out of the front door and stood just underneath Jane's open window talking angrily.

'Young puppy, I call him! Should like to give him a good thrashing. I couldn't speak, I was so angry, and Buggins more or less stood up for him, too. But I shall certainly write to Craig and tell him the sort of thing that's happening here.'

'Yes, I should. I think of writing to Madge myself about the goings-on. All in and out of each other's bedrooms and the gramophone playing till two and three in the morning. Then, another thing is, the servants won't stand it much longer, you know—champagne for breakfast, and so on! Mind you, the Monteaths aren't so bad. It's those other two. But that young man, my dear, he's *dreadful*.'

'Don't tell me. What d'you think he said to Brenda yesterday—didn't you hear? He said: "What a drenching colour your dress is!" Poor Brenda said afterwards: "Well, I've heard of drenching a cow!"'

'Yes, she told me. Well, I daresay we shall be able to laugh at all this when it's over, but I hardly find it amusing at the present moment, personally.'

'Oh, it's too shocking! It's the downfall of England, mind you . . . Mons! will you come here.'

At this moment the others came out, and climbing into the 'bus they all roared away up the drive. Jane lay in bed shaking with laughter, but she felt rather sorry for Sally and Walter. 'Still,' she thought, 'it can't be helped. We've done nothing wrong that I know of.'

She began slowly to dress, manicured her nails, took particular pains with her face and hair, and at about eleven she strolled downstairs. She looked into the billiard-room, half hoping that Albert would be there, but it was empty. Coming back into the hall she saw Sally sitting on the bottom step of the staircase.

'Oh, my dear, I'm feeling so awful!'

Jane dashed forward, put her arm round Sally's waist and half carried her to a sofa, where she went off into a dead faint. Jane, thoroughly alarmed, called out loudly for Walter, who ran downstairs in his dressing-gown.

'Oh, God!' he said on seeing Sally. 'What! She's not . . . ?'

'She's only fainted. Pull yourself together, Walter, and fetch some brandy or something. Look, though! she's coming round now.'

Sally opened her eyes and smiled at Walter, who was rubbing her hands in a distracted sort of way. Presently she sat up and drank some brandy, which Albert, appearing from nowhere, produced in a tumbler. Walter finished what she didn't want.

'Goodness, darling, what a turn you gave me! But what on earth's the matter with you? You were as right as rain a minute ago. D'you feel better now?'

'Yes, quite better, thank you. I'll just stay here for a bit, I think . . . Walter . . .'

'Yes, my angel.'

'Promise not to be cross.'

'Yes. What?'

'No, but promise really and truly.'

'Of course I promise, funny; but what is it?'

'Well, I'm afraid this means I'm in the family way. You're not cross? You see, I've been suspecting it for some time now and hoped for the best, you know; but this is rather conclusive, isn't it. Are you terribly shocked, my sweet?'

'No, naturally not, darling precious. But how careless of us. Never mind, I think it will be rather

109

sweet, really—I mean, the baby will. But it's too awful for you, though.'

'Oh, I don't mind. I am rather pleased. You are divine not to be cross. It is an anxiety all the same, isn't it, because how are we ever going to clothe the poor angel? I mean, babies' clothes are always covered with lace, just like underclothes. They must be frightfully expensive. Oh, gosh!'

'Well, my treasure, you'll have to be like pregnant women in books and sit with a quiet smile on your face making little garments. It is a bit of a shock at first, isn't it, the idea of your being a pregnant woman? But I suppose one will get used to it. Will it be a boy or a girl?'

'Both, perhaps.'

'*Really*, darling!'

'I mean twins, you idiot! But if not it'll be a girl, naturally: at least, I hope so.'

'You mustn't,' said Albert. 'I read somewhere that if you have been hoping for a girl and then it turns out to be a boy, it will have a nasty, perverted nature.'

'How awful! And does the opposite hold good?'

'Yes, I believe it does.'

'Oh, poor sweet: we must be careful. We'd better say "he" and "her" alternately: you couldn't call the angel "it", could you? You know I feel quite friendly towards him already. I think she will be a great comfort to us, Walter.'

'Yes, we were needing something to draw us together. Morris will be a bond between us.'

'Oh, need it be Maurice? It's not a name I have any feeling for.'

'M-o-r-r-i-s.' He spelt it out. 'If we call him that, we might get one free for an advertisement. You

110

never know your luck.'

'Why not Bentley, then, or Rolls?'

'No good. We couldn't afford to keep it up if we had one. Suppose the angel's a girl?'

'Minerva, and pop it. Morris Monteath: Minerva Monteath. Not at all bad.'

'Well, if we are going to do that, we'd better call her lots of things and have them all free. Minerva, Sanitas, Electrolux, Chubb, Ritz (then we could live there) Monteath. And I could think of dozens more.'

'Talking of living, where are we going to keep her: there's precious little room in the flat for him.'

'I can't think. What an awful idea!'

'I know,' said Walter, 'we can turn the cocktail chest into a cradle. My dear, what a good article for the Sunday Papers:

TURN YOUR COCKTAIL CHESTS INTO CRADLES!
England Needs More Babies
and
Fewer Cocktails!

———

PRACTICAL and PATRIOTIC.

No, but seriously, where do people keep their babies: one never does see them about, somehow.'

'I,' said Albert, 'am extremely shocked. I thought that when a woman discovered herself to be—well, "in an interesting condition," as they say in the papers, that she beckoned her husband into the conjugal bedroom and whispered shyly into his ear: "Baby's coming." I didn't know people went on like this, even in these days. I find it most painful

111

and disillusioning, and shall leave you to what should, in my opinion, be your confidences. In other words, you are a pair of clowns, and I must go and work. It's my great chance, as those Murgatroyds are out for the day and I shall have the billiard table to myself. I suppose I ought to congratulate you, Sally?'

He kissed her and left the room.

Jane had expected that he would ask her to go with him, but as he did not even look in her direction she forebore from suggesting it, and went for a dreary little walk alone till luncheon time.

*   *   *

During the next three days Albert completely neglected Jane, who was thrown into a state almost of frenzy by his behaviour. Ever since their midnight walk she had been eagerly awaiting an opportunity to tell him that she had now changed her mind, or rather that she knew her mind and was very definitely in love with him; but the opportunity did not come and it was Albert himself who prevented it. He not only took no particular notice of her, but actually went out of his way to avoid her.

Jane's natural reaction to this treatment was to appear more than indifferent and cold towards him, whereas really she was in a perfect fever wondering what could so have altered his feelings. She began to think she must have dreamt the whole affair.

On the third morning Albert announced that he was going to begin his portrait of Sally. Jane felt that this was almost more than she could stand. Ever since Sally's announcement of her pregnancy,

112

Albert had paid attention to no one else. He and Walter had sat with her for hours on end discussing what the baby would be like, whether it would grow up to be an artist or a writer: ('In point of fact, of course,' said Albert, 'he will probably be a well-known cricket pro.') how much Sally would suffer at the actual birth, and various other aspects of the situation; and Jane was beginning to feel if not exactly jealous, at any rate, very much left out in the cold.

The thought of them closeted together all day—Albert occupied with gazing at Sally's lovely face—was almost too much to bear. The fact that the Monteaths were completely wrapped up in each other was no consolation: it was more Albert's neglect of herself than his interest in Sally that was overwhelming her. She thought that she had never been so unhappy.

All day she avoided the billiard-room where Albert was painting. She tried to read, and write letters, but was too miserable to concentrate on anything. At luncheon Albert sat next to Sally and appeared unable to take his eyes from her face. Immediately the meal was over he carried her off to resume the sitting. Jane, too restless to remain indoors, wandered out towards the kitchen garden, where she came upon Lady Prague, with a large basket, cutting lavender. Any company seemed in her state of mind better than none and she offered to help. Lady Prague, giving her a pair of scissors, told her to cut the stalks long, and for some time they snipped away in silence. Presently Lady Prague said:

'If I were Walter Monteath I should be very much worried.'

'Why?' asked Jane, absent-mindedly.

'Well, it's rather obvious, isn't it? I mean, I don't want to make mischief, but one can't help seeing that Mr. Gates is violently in love with Sally, can one? And, if you ask me, I should say that she was more interested in him than she ought to be.'

Jane's heart stood still: she thought she was going to faint. All the suspicions which she had entertained, almost without knowing it, for the last two days turned in that black moment to certainties. Others beside herself had noticed: others more qualified to judge than she was were sure of it—therefore it was true!

She muttered some excuse to Lady Prague and ran back to the house, never pausing until she had reached her own room. She lay on the bed and sobbed her heart out. This seemed to do her a great deal of good; and when she had stopped crying, and had made herself look presentable again, she felt so calm and aloof that she decided to go into the billiard-room. She told herself that she would only make things worse by sulking and that the best thing would be to behave to Albert exactly as if none of this had happened.

There was an atmosphere of concentration in the billiard-room. Albert had dragged down from some attic a curious, stiff little Victorian sofa with curly legs, upholstered in wool and bead embroidery, and had posed Sally on this in front of the window with her feet up and her head turned towards the light. He was painting with great speed and enthusiasm. Walter was writing at a table near by. Neither looked round when Jane came in. Sally, however, was delighted to see her.

'Jane, darling, where have you been all this time?

We were beginning to think you must be getting off with the admiral. I hope, I'm sure, that his intentions are honourable, but don't marry him, darling. I feel he takes his eye out at night and floats it in Milton, which must look simply horrid. Anyway, I'm terribly glad you've come at last: these creatures have been just too boring and haven't thrown me a word all day. I've done nothing but contemplate that bust of the Prince Consort, and I'm terrified my poor angel will come out exactly like him—whiskers and all; because it's a well-known fact that pregnant women can influence their children's features by looking at something for too long. An aunt of mine could see from her bed a reproduction of the *Mona Lisa* and my wretched cousin is exactly like it—just that idiotic smile and muddy complexion—most depressing for her, poor thing.'

Jane laughed; but the joke about the admiral seemed unnecessary, she thought, and rather unkind considering the circumstances, forgetting that Sally was not aware of them. She wandered over to where Albert was painting and glanced at the canvas, not intending to make any comment. When she saw it, however, she was startled out of all her sulkiness into crying:

'But, surely, this isn't your style?'

'Not my usual style, no,' said Albert complacently, 'but one which, to my mind, expresses very well the personality of Sally. Do you agree?'

'Oh, Albert, it's too lovely! I can't tell you how much I admire it.' Her voice shook a little. ('Albert, Albert, darling, I do love you so much!')

The picture, which was small and square, was

115

painted with a curious precision of detail which gave it rather a Victorian aspect, but in spite of this the general design could have been achieved at no time but the present.

'It's nearly finished already, isn't it?'

'Very nearly, which is lucky, as I leave on Thursday for Paris.'

Jane felt as though somebody had hit her very hard and very suddenly in the middle of her chest. 'To-day is Tuesday ... He goes on Thursday ... Only one more day! Albert, oh, Albert darling! He doesn't love me, then: it's quite certain now that he doesn't; but he loves Sally, so he's running away. Lady Prague was right. But if he doesn't love me, why, why, did he pretend to? Only one more day!'

While all these thoughts were racing through Jane's head she was talking and laughing in the most natural way. Nobody could have suspected that she was in Hell.

Lady Prague came in, followed by Mr. Buggins.

'We've come to see this famous picture,' she said, walking up to it.

Albert, who hated the idea of Lady Prague criticizing his work, stood aside reluctantly.

('Only one more day!')

'How very sympathetic that is, Gates, or do I really mean *simpatica*?' said Mr. Buggins. 'I feel it to be so exactly right. I can't tell you how much I admire it, really too delightful.'

'Quite pretty,' said Lady Prague, half-shutting her eyes and putting her head on one side as she had learnt to do years ago at an art school in Paris. 'The face, of course, is a little out of drawing. But it's so difficult, isn't it,' she added, with an encouraging smile. 'And when you've once started

116

wrong it hardly ever comes right, does it? One fault, if I may say so, is that Mrs. Monteath has blue eyes, hasn't she? And there you can hardly tell what colour they're meant to be, can you? But perhaps your brushes are dirty.'

('Only one more day!')

CHAPTER THIRTEEN

Jane dressed for dinner that night with unusual care, even for her. She put on a white satin dress that she had not yet worn, feeling that it was a little too smart for a Scottish house party. With it she wore a short coat to match, trimmed with white fur. She spent almost an hour making up her face and looking in the glass before going downstairs, and felt that, at any rate, she appeared at her very best. This made her feel happier until she went into the drawing-room.

Albert was talking to Sally by the fire when Jane came in. He looked up for a moment and then, not rudely but as though unintentionally, he turned his back on her.

Jane felt that she would burst into tears, but, controlling herself, she talked in a loud, high voice to Walter until dinner was announced.

She sat between Admiral Wenceslaus and Captain Chadlington. The admiral poured a torrent of facts and figures relating to the freedom of the sea into her all but deaf ears. She caught the words: 'Prize Courts ... Foreign Office ... Nearly two millions ... International law ... Page ... Permanent officials ... Blockade.' ... And said: 'No' ... 'Yes'

... and 'Not really?' from time to time in as intelligent a voice as she could muster.

When the grouse was finished she was left to the mercies of Captain Chadlington, which meant that she could indulge in her own thoughts until the end of the meal. He had given up asking what pack she hunted with in despair, and that was his only conversational gambit. Albert was sitting next to Sally again and Jane hardly even minded this. She was worn out with her emotions.

After dinner Lady Prague suggested 'Lists.' Sally said she was tired and would go to bed. Walter settled down to the piano, and Albert pleaded that he had work to do.

'Very well, if nobody wants to play we might as well go and listen to the wireless.'

'It's a wonderful programme to-night,' said the general. 'A talk on how wire-netting is made from A to B—Z, I mean—and selections from *The Country Girl*. I wouldn't miss it for anything.'

They all left the room except Walter, who was playing some Brahms, and Jane and Albert who stood by the fire laughing.

'Why are you going away so soon?' she asked him, almost against her will.

'I am wasting time here. I must return to Paris,' he said. And then, abruptly: 'Come with me. I've something to show you.'

Jane's heart thumped as she followed him into the billiard-room.

Albert shut the door and looking at her in a peculiar way, his head on one side, he said:

'Well?'

Jane put up her face to be kissed.

'Darling, Albert!'

118

He took her in his arms and kissed her again and again.

'Oh, Albert! I was so miserable. I thought you'd stopped loving me.'

'Yes, I know. I meant you to.'

'Oh, you monster! Why?'

'Because it was the only way for you to make up your mind. I won't be kept on a string by any woman.'

'But I'd made it up completely after that walk. Yes, it's no good shaking your head. I had, and I was going to tell you as soon as I got a chance to. Oh, *darling*, how I do love you!'

'Come and sit here.'

Jane put her head on his shoulder. She had never been so happy.

'When did you fall in love with me?'

'The first time I saw you at Sally's.'

'Did you? Fancy, I thought you seemed so bored.'

'How beautiful you are!'

'Am I?'

'Don't say "Am I?" like that, it's disgusting. Yes you are—very!'

'Oh, *good*. Albert?'

'Yes?'

'Shall I come and live with you in Paris?'

'Well, wives quite often *do* live with their husbands, you know, for a bit, anyhow.'

Jane sat up and stared at him.

'Do you want to marry me?'

'But, of course, you funny child. What d'you imagine I want?'

'I don't know. I thought you might like me to be

119

your mistress. I never really considered marrying you.'

'Good gracious, darling! What d'you suppose I am? An ordinary seducer?'

Jane grew rather pink; it sounded unattractive, somehow, put like that.

'And may I ask if you're in the habit of being people's mistress?'

'Well, no, actually I'm not. But I should love to be yours. Albert, don't be so childish. Have you *no* modern ideas?'

'Not where you're concerned, I'm afraid.'

'I don't think I believe in marriage.'

'Now you're being childish. Anyway, why don't you?'

'Well, none of my friends have made a success of it, except Walter and Sally, and they're such very special people.'

'So are we very special people. If you can't make a success of marriage you're no more likely to make a success of living together. In any case, I insist on being married, and I'm the grown-up one here, please, remember.'

'I'm not so sure. Still I expect it would be rather nice, and I do look terribly pretty in white tulle. You'll have to meet my family, in that case, you know. You're not really going to Paris?'

'No, of course not—now. Let's stay here for a bit and then we'll go and see your parents. Will they disapprove of me?'

'I expect so, most probably,' said Jane hopefully. She had refused to marry at least two people she was quite fond of, on the grounds that her family would be certain to approve of them. 'They simply hate artists. But we need never see them once we're married.'

'I think that would be dreadful,' said Albert. 'After all, you are their only child, think how they will miss you. I shall have to spare you to them occasionally.'

'Darling, how sweet you are! Have you ever had a mistress?'

'Two.'

'Do you love me as much as them?'

'I might in time.'

'Will you love me for ever?'

'No, I shouldn't think so. It doesn't happen often.'

'Do you love me a lot?'

'Yes I do. A great lot.'

'When shall we be married?'

'After my exhibition, about the end of November.'

'Where shall we live?'

'Somewhere abroad. Paris, don't you think? I'll go back and find a flat while you're buying your trousseau, or you could come, too, and buy it there.'

'Albert, you're such a surprise to me. I should have imagined that you were the sort of person who would like to be married in the morning, and never think of a trousseau.'

'Well, my angel, you know how I hate getting up, and after all, I've got to see your underclothes, haven't I? No, I'm all for having a grand wedding I must say; one gets more presents like that, too.'

'My dear, you've never seen any wedding presents or you wouldn't call that an advantage.'

'Still, I suppose they're marketable?'

'Shall we be frightfully poor?'

'Yes, fairly poor. I have just over a thousand a

121

year besides what I make.'

'And I've four hundred. Not too bad. Walter and Sally have to manage on a thousand between them. I must say they're generally in the deep end, though. I simply can't think what they'll do now, poor sweets. How soon shall I tell my family?'

'Not till we leave here, if I were you. You might change your mind.'

'Yes, I quite expect I shall do that. We won't tell the Murgatroyds, either, will we? Just Walter and Sally.'

'Yes, I think so.'

'How many children shall we have?'

'Ten?'

'Albert! You can consider that our engagement is at an end.'

'About four, really. Of course, you may have three lots of triplets like Lady Prague in the Consequences.'

'You do love me, don't you?'

'Yes, I do. How many more times?'

'As many as I like. You know I'm very glad I came to Scotland.'

'So am I. Come on, funny, d'you realize it's past one; we must go to bed or there'll be a hideous scandal.'

CHAPTER FOURTEEN

The days which followed were spent by Jane and Albert in a state of idyllic happiness. It was quite easy to keep their engagement a secret from all but the Monteaths as the heartier members of the house party were so seldom indoors; when there was no shooting to occupy them they would be fishing or playing tennis. The evenings were no longer brightened by the inevitable 'Lists'; nobody dared to thwart Lady Prague by refusing to play, but at least Albert, who could bear it no longer, read out a list of diseases so shocking and nauseating that the affronted peeress took herself off to the study and the game was never resumed.

One day they were all having tea in the great hall. This was an important meal for the shooters, who ate poached eggs and scones and drank out of enormous cups reminiscent of a certain article of bedroom china ware. Albert, who detested the sight of so much swilling, seldom attended it, preferring to have a cup of weak China tea or a cocktail sent into the billiard-room, but on this occasion he had come in to ask Walter something and had stayed on talking to Jane.

'Tomorrow,' said Mr. Buggins to the company at large, 'there are to be some very good Highland games at Invertochie which is about thirty miles from here. I have been talking to the general and he sees no reason why we shouldn't all go over to them. There are two cars, his own and Craig's Rolls-Royce, so there'll be plenty of room if everyone would like to come. We think it would be advisable to take a picnic luncheon which we could eat on the way at a very well-known beauty spot called the Corbie's Egg.'

There was a murmur of assent and 'That will be lovely,' from the assembled guests.

'The Corbie,' went on Mr. Buggins, 'is the local name for a crow. It is not known how that particular mountain came to be called the Corbie's

123

Egg, but the name is an ancient one: I came across it once in a sixteenth-century manuscript.'

Mr. Buggins's audience began to fade away. The 'grown-ups,' as Albert called them, were frankly bored by folk-lore, which, it is only fair to add, was already well known to them, they had all been fellow-guests with Mr. Buggins before. The others, who had not, politely listened to a long and rather dreary account of how he, personally, was inclined to think that sacrifices might have taken place on the mountain at some prehistoric date, first of human beings, then, when people were becoming more humane, of animals, and finally the whole thing having degenerated into mere superstition, of a Corbie's Egg.

'I do hope you will all come to the games,' he added rather wistfully. 'Of course, I know you don't really much like that sort of thing, but I feel that it would be a great pity for you to leave the Highlands without having seen this typical aspect of national life. And it would make my day very much more pleasant if you came. We could all pack into the Rolls, and the others could drive with the general in his Buick.'

Mr. Buggins had so evidently been thinking it all out and was so pathetically anxious for them to go, that the Monteaths, Albert and Jane, who had each inwardly been planning a happy day without the grown-ups, were constrained to say that there was nothing they would enjoy so much, that they adored picnics, and could hardly wait to see the Corbie's Egg, let alone the Highland games.

'And what games do they play?' asked Albert.

'Actually, in the usual sense of the word, no games. It is what you would call in the South,

124

sports.' (Mr. Buggins identified himself so much with the North that he was apt to forget that he also was a mere Englishman. He had once seriously contemplated adding his grandmother's maiden name to his own and calling himself Forbes-Buggins.) 'The programme consists of dancing, piping, tossing the caber, and such things. The chieftains of the various neighbouring clans act as judges. It is all most interesting.'

'It must be,' said Albert. 'I long to see the chieftains.'

At dinner the subject was once more discussed at some length, and it was finally decided that the whole party should go, starting punctually at half-past twelve; and Lady Prague, who to Sally's great relief had taken upon herself all questions of housekeeping, gave the necessary orders for a picnic luncheon.

The next morning at twelve o'clock Albert had not put in an appearance, and kind Mr. Buggins, knowing his customary lateness and aware that Lady Prague and General Murgatroyd wait for no man, went to his bedroom to see if he had awakened.

Albert was sitting on the edge of his bed, wearing a pair of exquisite sprigged pyjamas. A gramophone blared out 'The Ride of the Valkyries'; the whole room smelt strongly of gardenias. He stopped the gramophone and said:

'This is a great pleasure, Mr. Buggins. So early, too; your energy never ceases to amaze me. I am in a state of intense excitement. Look what I received this morning from a friend in London.' He held out a Victorian glass paper-weight.

'Look into it carefully.'

Mr. Buggins did so, and was immediately rewarded by the sight of Gladstone's memorable features.

'Now,' said Albert excitedly, 'turn it round just a little.'

Mr. Buggins obeyed, and lo and behold! Mr. Gladstone changed before his very eyes to Mr. Disraeli. He made a suitable exclamation of gratified surprise.

'It is unique!' cried Albert. 'Unique in the iconographie of Gladstone and Disraeli and also as a paper-weight. I regard it as a find of the greatest significance.'

'Very interesting. To what date do you think it belongs?'

'Mr. Buggins, I have a theory about that paper-weight; but this, of course, is just my own idea, and must not be taken too seriously, as I am by no means an infallible authority on the subject, though it is one which I have studied deeply. You have guessed, of course, that I refer to Gabelsburgher.'

Mr. Buggins had guessed no such thing, but he bowed courteously.

'In other words, I believe this paper-weight to be an original Gabelsburgher. It will, of course, be some time before I shall be able to proclaim this as an established fact. You ask what date it is? I reply that if, as I think, it is by the hand of the master, it would almost certainly have been made between the years 1875 and 1878. Gabelsburgher, as you know, came to England for the first time in '75. In '76 Elsie was taken ill, in '78 he laid her remains in the Paddington cemetery and came away a broken man. Many of his best paper-weights were buried with

126

his beloved, and from that time his work deteriorated beyond recognition. It is easy to see that this jewel belongs to his very greatest period, and I should myself be inclined to think that it was created in the March or April of '76 while Elise was still in the heyday of her youth and beauty. But, as I said just now, I am very far from infallible.'

Mr. Buggins, who knew nothing and cared less about Gabelsburgher, and who heard the cars arriving at the front door, became a little restive during this speech, repeating at the end of it:

'Very interesting. I really came to tell you that we start in about ten minutes for the Highland games.'

'Ah! good gracious! I had quite forgotten!' cried Albert, leaping out of bed and seizing his black taffeta dressing-gown. 'But have no fear, I shall not be late.'

Albert, Walter, Mr. Buggins, Jane and Sally went in the first car, the Craigdallochs' Rolls-Royce, and with them, as they had the most room, was packed the luncheon: one large picnic basket, two thermos flasks and several bottles of beer and whisky.

In the general's Buick, which he drove himself and which was to start a few minutes later than the Rolls, were Lady Prague, the Chadlingtons and Admiral Wenceslaus. Lord Prague was in the apparently moribund condition which characterized him on non-shooting days, and stayed behind.

The Rolls-Royce drove along with a pleasantly luxurious motion. Mr. Buggins pointed out many places of interest as they passed through typical Highland scenery, among others the 'banksome brae' where 'Ronnie waur killed i' the ficht,' and the lodge gates of Castle Bane, let at present to

127

some rich Americans who had installed (Mr. Buggins shook his head sadly) a cocktail bar in the chief dungeon. Sally was much excited to hear this and wondered if it would be possible to make their acquaintance.

'I should so *love* to see the inside of Castle Bane!' she cried. 'And I simply *worship dungeons*, of course!'

'I believe the public are admitted every Thursday, but I will make inquiries,' said Mr. Buggins.

Presently the Rolls-Royce arrived at the Corbie's Egg, a large yellowish mountain commanding an interminable prospect of other mountains, valleys, streams and pine woods. They all got out of the car and were induced by Mr. Buggins, an ardent picnicker, to drag the hamper, rugs, and bottles half-way up a sort of precipice, the idea being that they would thus enjoy a slightly better view. What, however, they gained in that respect they lost in comfort, as they were perched on a decided slope and had some difficulty in preventing basket and bottles from slipping down it.

Having unpacked the luncheon they waited politely for the others; but when a quarter of an hour passed by with no signs of the Buick, Sally suggested that they should begin. 'I'm pretty peckish,' she said, 'eating for two now, you see.'

Albert remarked that the Murgatroyds certainly would not have waited for them, and they all fell upon the food, munching away in a happy silence.

It was only when they had quite finished and were drinking their coffee with the delicious feeling, so rare at picnics, that even if there were any more food it would be difficult to eat it, that

128

Sally noticed, to her extreme horror, that there was absolutely nothing left for the others.

She announced this fact in a voice shaking with hysteria. There was a ghastly silence.

Mr. Buggins said: 'Surely they are bringing their own,' without much conviction.

'No,' wailed Sally, 'this was for everybody.'

Another silence. Walter tried to speak, but no words came. Mr. Buggins gulped down some neat whisky and said:

'Wait a minute. We'll see what's left. Hum—yes, one leg of grouse. Three tongue sandwiches. Look! What's this? A packet of something! Oh dear! Petit-Beurre biscuits, rather cold comfort. Fourteen apples (curious how the cook here seems to think we are all fruitarians). No beer at all. Half a bottle of whisky. A thermos of hot milk. Yes, this is very awkward indeed.'

Another dreadful silence descended upon them. Sally wrung her hands in despair.

'Oh, goodness, goodness me! What *are* we to do?'

Albert poured the remains of the whisky down his throat. Suddenly he shouted:

'I know, of course! The only thing we can do is to hide the picnic basket and pretend it fell out of the car. Quick! quick! before they come!'

With shaking hands and furtive glances down the road they packed the debris of their lunch into the picnic basket, which they proceeded to hide between two large boulders. They then seized the rugs and scrambled down a precipitous slope to the motor-car, explaining matters rather breathlessly to the bewildered chauffeur, who, when he grasped what they were driving at, was only too pleased to aid and abet their little plan as he had a private

129

grudge against the general.

Hardly were all these preparations completed when the Buick bore down upon them and drew up just behind the Rolls-Royce.

General Murgatroyd was the first one to get out and walked briskly up to where the guilty ones were waiting by the roadside. He looked hot and cross, his hands were covered with oil.

'How's this?' he said in a loud angry voice. 'We thought at least you'd have the lunch all ready for us by now. We've had a beastly time with a slipping clutch. Got it put right now but it's been the hell of a journey, I can tell you, and, personally, I'm ready for my food. Come on, let's get it out.'

There was a gloomy silence. At last Walter, prodded from behind by Sally, cleared his throat and said:

'I'm afraid, sir, that a rather—er—disappointing thing has happened to the lunch. Albert found that there wasn't quite enough room for his legs with the basket on the floor of the car, so we stopped and put it on to the carrier. When we arrived here we found to our dismay that it had disappeared—it must have dropped off as we drove along. We hoped that you might perhaps have come across it and picked it up. No such luck, I suppose?'

'This is damned annoying,' said the general violently. 'Who strapped it on to the carrier?'

'Albert and I did, sir.'

'Then you must have done it damned inefficiently, that's all I can say.'

He glared at Albert.

The admiral here came forward and said, not unkindly:

'Well, it can't be helped now. Let's have a drink

130

while we're waiting.'

'Unfortunately, sir, the bottles seem to have been forgotten. I thought when I woke up this morning that Friday the 13th is seldom a lucky day.'

'It happens to be Friday the 12th to-day, though,' said Lady Prague.

The admiral at first appeared stunned by this piece of news, but, suddenly galvanized into life, he cried:

'Forgotten! What do you mean? I saw them into the car myself. I always see to the drinks.'

'Yes, he does: I can vouch for that.' The general looked again at Albert as he spoke.

Nobody answered.

'This is all most peculiar and extremely annoying,' said Lady Prague. 'What makes it worse is that the picnic-basket with fittings was Prague's silver-wedding present from the tenants—with his first wife, of course. We shall certainly have to inform the police of this loss. Meanwhile, what shall we do for luncheon?'

'If I might make a suggestion, Lady Prague,' ventured Mr. Buggins timidly, 'perhaps you had better go to the Auld Lang Syne at Invertochie and have your luncheon there?'

'And what about all of you? Aren't you hungry?'

'Yes, indeed, we are starving—starving. I meant, of course, for all of us to go, but thought that if only a few can get in, owing to the large crowd which is always attracted there by the games, that you should in justice come before us, as it was partly owing to our carelessness that the basket was lost.'

'Oh, I see; yes. Well, there's no point in waiting here, we might as well push on to the Auld Lang Syne. Most inconvenient and tiresome.'

They all climbed back into the cars and when they were once more under way, Albert said:

'Really, Walter, you are a sneak. Why did you say it was my legs that hadn't enough room: surely you could have chosen someone else. I'm in such disfavour with the general and I feel now that he will never look on me kindly again.'

'I'm sorry; I couldn't think of anyone else.'

'Well, there was yourself.'

'I never think of myself.'

'I suppose you all realize,' said Jane, who was tightly holding Albert's hand under the rug, 'that we are fated to eat another enormous lunch. Personally, I couldn't face a small biscuit at the moment.'

They gazed at each other in horror at this prospect, but Mr. Buggins assured them that there was no need for anxiety as the hotel was certain to be full on that particular day.

'I am even rather perturbed,' he added, 'as to whether those poor hungry things will get a bite or sup.'

'I'm quite sure that Lady Prague will get a bite, and don't doubt that the admiral will somehow find a sup,' said Albert; 'but think how awful it would be if there did happen to be enough for all of us. Hadn't we better pretend to have a breakdown and let the others go on?'

'You forget it's the general behind us, who obviously knows all about cranking plugs and things: he'd see in a moment that nothing was wrong. No, we shall have to risk it.'

When they arrived at the Auld Lang Syne it presented, to their dismay, a singularly empty and welcoming appearance.

132

'Lunch for ten? Certainly. This way, please.'

The waiter led them through a stuffy little hall bedecked with stags' heads, up some brown linoleum stairs to the dining-room which, though empty, smelt strongly of humanity.

'No, sir; no crowd now. There has been, sir; oh, yes, but they're all to the games. Will you start with fish or soup, sir?'

At this moment the rest of the party appeared, headed by Lady Prague, who said:

'As we are in such a hurry I will order for everybody,' and took the menu card from the waiter.

'Tomato soup, roast mutton, two vegetables, rice pudding and prunes, Cheddar cheese, celery and biscuits. That will do nicely. I shall drink ginger beer. What about everybody else?'

'Whisky,' said the admiral quickly. 'I wish I could understand what happened to those bottles.'

He looked suspiciously at Albert.

Very soon the tomato soup arrived. It tasted strongly and unnaturally of tomatoes, was hot, thick and particularly filling. Lady Prague fell upon it with relish and crumbled bread into it.

Albert, Jane, Walter, Sally and Mr. Buggins never forgot that lunch. Seated in a row, their eyes fixed upon a print of the Battle of Khandi Pass (underneath which hung a key so that the members of the British aristocracy portrayed there should easily be recognizable), they miserably waded through the bill of fare ordered by Lady Prague.

They suffered.

First the soup, followed by enormous helpings of congealing mutton with boiled vegetables; then—except for Albert—mountains of tepid rice

133

pudding floating about in brown prune juice and studded with the prunes. Albert firmly refused this, saying:

'It is my peculiar misfortune that from a child I have been unable to digest rice. Prunes I find so disintegrating that I seldom touch them.'

'Traitor!' whispered Jane, kicking him under the table.

'No biscuits, thank you,' said Mr. Buggins; adding in a jocular voice, 'I have always been told that one should rise from a meal ready to eat a penny bun.'

'And are you ready to now?' asked Albert doubtfully.

At last the nauseating meal drew to a close, and Walter (who luckily had some money with him) was obliged to put down twenty-eight shillings for his own, Sally's, Jane's and Albert's share of the bill. This was felt by some to be the saddest moment of the day.

'My spirit is broken,' said Albert, as they walked downstairs again, 'or I should certainly bargain with the innkeeper for that exquisite aspidistra. I covet it. But I have no energy left in me for such exertions. Mr. Buggins, do tell me, I have always so much wanted to know, who *was* Auld Lang Syne?'

*　　*　　*

It was past three o'clock when they arrived at the enclosure where the games were taking place. Each member of the party had to pay five shillings to go in.

'I knew it would be cheaper, in the end, to go to the Lido,' said Walter bitterly.

134

There was an enormous crowd in the enclosure consisting of very strong-looking people; the men mostly wore kilts and the women dull but serviceable tweeds.

Albert bought a programme which he shared with Jane. It was printed on thin pink paper and informed them that they were about to witness:

TUG OF WAR. VAULTING WITH POLE.
PIPING. DANCING.
THROWING THE HAMMER. TOSSING THE CABER.
FOOT RACES. CYCLE RACES. RELAY TEAM RACES.
PIPING COMPETITION.

Albert began explaining this to Jane as they were separated from the others:

'"Tossing the caber". Now that will be worth seeing; the caber is Scottish for a young bull and this ancient sport was introduced into Scotland by the survivors of the Spanish Armada, who settled in many of the islands. "Throwing the hammer". Two men, I believe, are given six hammers each to throw and they see who can knock out the other one first. Dangerous, but what is that to these wild clansmen?'

'How d'you know all this?' asked Jane suspiciously.

'My dear, of course I know all about it. Don't be tiresome, but come and see for yourself.'

As they drew near to the arena their ears were greeted by a curious medley of sounds, the results of two brass bands playing different tunes, a band of bagpipes and a man walking drearily round alone, piping.

'So like *Le Pas d'Acier*,' murmured Albert, who

135

had long entertained an unreasonable dislike for that ballet.

The arena, which was railed off from the crowd by ropes, was a large piece of flat ground like a football field. At one side of it there was a raised platform, on which sat several ancient men in kilts.

'The chieftains,' Albert explained, 'of neighbouring clans. Although they look so friendly, each in reality is fingering his dirk; their hearts are black with age-old hatreds of each other. Meanwhile, their brave clansmen are striving with might and main to win the games. Let's get up closer, I can't see anything.'

The arena presented an extraordinary spectacle of apparently meaningless activity. People seemed to be doing things quite by themselves in every available corner of the field, while, encircling the whole, about seven skinny little men in shorts were quickly cycling round and round, followed by a crowd of even skinnier little men, running. They mostly looked like Whitechapel Jews. Some girls in Highland dress and long flowing hair were dancing a fling in one corner; in another an enormous giant appeared to be balancing a tree on his chest. The tug-of-war went on the whole time, neither side gaining an inch, and the vaulting also was incessant.

'I am bitterly disappointed!' cried Albert, when he had gazed for some time upon this medley of sports. 'I had imagined that I was going to see savage Highlanders, in philabeg and bonnet, performing unheard-of feats. And what do I find? Men of more insignificant physique than myself cycling, running, jumping, and doing it rather worse than little boys at their private school sports. As for the noise, I cannot condemn it too heartily. I am suffering real physical pain and, also, I feel most dreadfully sick.'

'Well, can you wonder?' said Jane. 'Personally, I've never felt so ill in my life before. What I'm wondering, though, is how we are to account for the picnic-basket being found again.'

'Oh, easily. We can say that some rough man brought it back.'

'Yes, but that's so unlikely; because how is the rough man to know whom it belongs to? Presumably, if there is an address inside, it will be that of the Prague home, as they say in films.'

'We shall have to advertise for it. Oh! the boredom of these games! I've never known anything so oppressive. And as for those *cyclistes* they make me feel positively giddy, round and round like rats in a cage. Can't we go home soon? There's Alfred Sprott! Doesn't he look awfully jolly? Let's go and embarrass him.'

Albert gracefully approached Lord Alfred, who was standing with a pretty blonde young woman.

'De-ar Alfred,' he said, placing a hand on his shoulder, 'why are you not playing in these delightful games? I remember so well the day you won *all* the sports at Eton.'

Lord Alfred turned scarlet, muttered something, and hurried away into the crowd.

'Always so *gauche*, the darling boy,' said Albert sadly. 'Here comes Mr. Buggins.'

Mr. Buggins was walking with a tall, oldish man in a kilt, whom he introduced as Sir Alexander McDougal.

'Sir Alexander,' he said, 'is the convener of the games this year. He has just been judging the piping competition.'

137

'In other words, I suppose,' said Albert, 'the producer. Well, sir, I must congratulate you. Seen as a sort of out-door ballet these games must command the highest praise. The music, too, although at first unmelodious, seems now a very fitting background to these fantastic gestures. Charming! Charming!'

Sir Alexander walked quickly away, followed by Mr. Buggins.

'Why did you say that,' asked Jane (a truthful girl), 'when you know how bored you are feeling?'

'Well, darling, I always think that any artistic endeavour, however unsuccessful, should be encouraged. These games do show a certain amount of enterprise; when looked at impartially there is a sort of pattern to be discerned in them. In time they might become most interesting and unique. Meanwhile, they are, of course, far too monotonous.'

'And do you realize,' said Walter, who, with Sally, now joined them, 'that they are still doing the very things that they were doing at ten o'clock this morning?'

'The same people?'

'The same, or others so similar to them as to be indistinguishable.'

'Don't you think,' said Sally wearily, 'that we might go home, as we're all here?'

This suggestion was felt to meet the situation quite admirably, and Walter was sent off to find Mr. Buggins, while the others waited in the car.

'Sicker,' said Albert, as they finally bowled off towards Dalloch Castle, 'I have never felt.'

After dinner that evening the party assembled in the hall to take leave of Captain and Lady Brenda

138

Chadlington, who, to nobody's very great regret, were leaving the castle for the jolly cosy little lodge where Lord Alfred Sprott and others made such a cheery crowd. When they had gone the butler came up to Lady Prague and informed her that the picnic-basket had just been brought back by a rough man.

'Most peculiar,' said Lady Prague; but she let the matter rest at that.

CHAPTER FIFTEEN

Jane sat talking to Sally in her bedroom after tea. Poor Sally had spent most of the day being sick. Morris (or Minerva) was beginning to make his (or her) presence felt in no uncertain terms.

'What is so unfair,' she said, 'is that I'm not only sick in the morning, which one expects to be, but sick in the afternoon and evening as well. However, I'm quite pleased we're going to have him, you know. I think a little squawking baby will be great fun, and Walter's been divine about it.'

'Albert and I are going to have four, all boys. One thing I'm *not* looking forward to is telling my family about Albert. Think of their feelings when they hear that he's an artist, who lives abroad and was sent down from Oxford. They'll blow up, that's all. Oh, how I dread it!'

Sally, who knew that Jane enjoyed nothing so much as a scene with her parents, murmured words of sympathy.

'I expect they'll be delighted when they see him. Albert gets on very well with older people. Look at

139

Mr. Buggins.'

'Yes, and look at General Murgatroyd,' said Jane quickly, frowning at the idea that they might approve of Albert. 'He's much more like daddy than Mr. Buggins is.'

'My dear Jane, how absurd you are! Two people couldn't be more different than Sir Herbert and General Murgatroyd. Your father has a great sense of humour, for one thing, and then he's a very cultivated man. Anyhow, you shouldn't talk like that: you get all your brains from him.'

'No, indeed, I don't. I get them from my maternal grandmother, Judith Trevor. Brains often skip a generation, you know, and come out in the grandchildren. Poor mummy and daddy are both terribly stupid: darlings, of course, but narrow-minded and completely unintellectual.'

'I simply don't understand your attitude towards your parents, and, what's more, I believe the whole thing is a pose. Why, when you're at home you always seem to be so fond of them, and anyone can see that they adore you.'

'Think what you like, my dear Sally, you won't alter the truth. Of course, I know how charming they are and how grateful I ought to be for everything they've done, and so on, and in a way I am fond of them. We have a different outlook and that's all there is to it.'

The door opened and Walter came in with a telegram in his hand.

'Too extraordinary,' he said. 'Here's a wire from Ralph to say that he and Mrs. Fairfax are coming to dinner. Can you understand it?'

Sally read it out loud:

140

May Loudie and I come to dinner to-day? Will arrive about eight on chance of finding you.

RALPH

'How very mysterious! Why are they in Scotland?'

'I know, so peculiar and why together? However, we shall hear all about it this evening. How pleased Albert will be to see Ralph. Do you imagine they'll be wanting to stay the night?'

'Certainly, I should think. We'll get rooms ready in case. Anyway, it's very exciting. I'm always pleased to see Ralph, myself, and Mrs. Fairfax is such heaven. But I'm longing to know what it all means, aren't you?'

'What *will* the Murgatroyds think of Mrs. Fairfax?'

'I expect they probably know her already. But I imagine that Ralph will be a bit of a shock to them.'

'Oh, this is going to be fun!' said Jane, and she ran off to tell Albert.

Dinner was well advanced before there was any sign of the newcomers.

As Sally had conjectured, Mrs. Fairfax was well-known to all the Murgatroyds. A much-married lady, she had in turn been the wife of an English duke, an American millionaire and an Italian prince; and now, in theory, if not in fact, shared the bed of a rather depressing Colonel Fairfax. Lady Prague, in common with many of her contemporaries, still remained on bowing terms with her despite these moral lapses; as the mother of an English marquess, an American heiress and an Italian duke, Mrs. Fairfax could always command a certain measure of tolerance even from the most strait-laced dowagers.

Lady Prague was in the middle of explaining to the general that dear Louisa had always been such a high-spirited girl and could, therefore, hardly be blamed for her actions. 'Not that I approve of her, of course. I don't, but somehow one forgives things to her that one couldn't put up with in others'—when the door opened and Ralph Callendar swayed into the room. He kissed Sally's hand, blew kisses to Jane and Albert, bowed to the rest of the company, and explained:

'Loudie is making up her face in the hall. She thinks that she's looking tired, but that if she is sufficiently *maquillée* everyone will think: "How painted she is!" instead of: "How aged she is!" which is naturally preferable. The angel! Here she comes!'

The door opened again to admit an immensely fat Pekinese, with bulging eyes and a rolling gait, followed by his mistress and human counterpart, Mrs. Fairfax. Short and plump, waddling rather than walking, her little round face inches deep in paint, her little fat hands covered with rings, her stout little body enveloped in a sable coat, she resembled nothing so much as a rather prepossessing giant Pekinese. The moment she was inside the room she let loose a perfect flow of inconsequent chatter:

'Sally, darling, what *must* you think of us, forcing ourselves on you like this? We heard you were here quite by chance and couldn't resist coming. Florence, what a surprise! And Mowbray, too, and the admiral, and dear, nice Mr. Buggins! Albert such an age since I've seen you. Jane—looking so beautiful. What's happened to you, my dear? In

142

love, I suppose, as usual? Well, I must say this is a delightful party. And the poor Craigdallochs are away, I hear.'

She sat down next to Walter and continued:

'Of course, I suppose you all think Ralph and I are eloping? Well, no. Though to be frank, this is the first time I've made a journey of the sort without eloping. I ran away with all my dear husbands, you know, even with poor Cosmo, though I can't remember why that was necessary. Oh, yes, of course I know, I was under age and my father said we must wait for three months. Three months! As though anyone could. So we just ran away to Paris: only for a night and it was all most innocent (dear Cosmo—so pompous!); but we were seen by several people—we took care to be, of course—and after that it was plain sailing and we were married in the rue d'Aguesso, I remember. Really, it made a vivid impression on me at the time. The Ambassador was there and poor father gave me away, and poor Cosmo took me away, dear thing, to Rome or somewhere, and it was all very different from what I had expected. And now I've shocked Florence. But what was I talking about? Oh, yes, of course. Well, Ralph and I are not eloping: merely escaping.'

'Escaping?'

'From Linda May. From the West Coast of Scotland really. You tell them about it, darling, while I get on with my fish.'

'You see,' said Ralph, shutting his pained eyes and speaking in a voice which gave the impression that he had lived a thousand tiring lives, 'Linda, the poppet, seems to have gone mad. It is a great tragedy. She invited us to go for a cruise in her

143

yacht. She said we would go to the Islands. Naturally thinking she meant the Greek islands, we accepted, intending to leave her quite soon for the Lido. Two days before we were to start I discovered, to my horror and amazement, that we were being taken to visit some islands on the West Coast of Scotland. Well, you know, Albert, Scotland is all right for you, but it's not my *period*. So I telephoned to Loudie and told her this agonizing news. I begged her to come straight to the Lido instead. But no, obstinate as a mule. She insisted on going with Linda. Imagine my mental sufferings faced with the prospect either of not seeing Loudie for weeks, or of facing these ghastly hardships in her company. I begged, I implored her to change her mind; and when, at last, I realized that she was absolutely bent upon going, I made the great sacrifice and accompanied her. But I did beg, didn't I, Loudie?'

'Yes, darling, you did, indeed,' she replied, with her mouth full.

'To continue: It was even more horrible than I had anticipated. The scenery—my dear Albert—forgive me if I say that the scenery made one feel physically sick whenever the eye strayed out of the porthole. I kept my curtain drawn all day and even then I couldn't help seeing those mountains sometimes—they haunted me. To make matters worse, Linda, it appears, is madly in love with a monster of a Scotsman, who came to dinner last night in his kilt. Those hairy old knees decided us. "The mountains I can bear," said Loudie. "Natives in the semi-nude at dinner-time is another matter. I leave to-morrow." Luckily the angel had her Austro-Daimler sitting at Oban, so here we are!

144

But I tell you—'

At this moment there was a piercing shriek from Lady Prague. The Pekinese was seen to have his teeth firmly embedded in her right ankle.

'Doglet!' said Mrs. Fairfax in a gently reproving voice, '*what* do I see you doing, my own? Somebody give him a piece of grouse and he'll leave go at once.'

General Murgatroyd, however, seized the dog roughly by its tail, whereupon it turned round and bit him in the hand. The general shook it off and, crimson with rage, demanded that it should instantly be destroyed.

'My little Doglet destroyed? Oh, what a dreadful idea! Such a horrid word, too. You cruel old general! Besides, a dog is always allowed his first bite, by law, isn't he?'

'First fiddlesticks! Anyhow, it's had two bites this evening—Florence and myself. The animal is not safe, I tell you.'

'"The animal," indeed! Fancy calling my Doglet "the animal"! Come here, my precious. The general isn't safe: he wants to *destroy* you. Ralph dear, be an angel and put Doglet in the car, will you, till after dinner? Thank you so much. I do hope you're not hurt, Florence?'

'Yes, Louise, the skin *is* broken and he has torn my stocking rather badly. A new pair! Of course it doesn't signify. I must go and paint it with iodine. I only trust the animal has not got hydrophobia.'

She left the room angrily, General Murgatroyd opening the door for her with a gesture of exaggerated chivalry. Lord Prague, who had noticed nothing, went on eating.

'I'm so sorry that Doglet should have caused all

this commotion,' said Mrs. Fairfax. 'The angel! So unlike him! I've never known him really to lose his temper before, but you wouldn't believe how sensitive he is to dress. I ought to have remembered that pink georgette is the one material he simply cannot abide. In fact, all georgette is inclined to upset him; and dear Florence's shoes, with those long pointed toes, would drive him distracted. Poor little sweet! He'll be utterly miserable after this, I'm afraid.'

'And he'd have reason to be if I had anything to do with him,' muttered the general.

'You must find this house very interesting, Albert,' said Ralph, returning from his mission. 'So exactly your period.'

'Indeed, yes, I do,' replied Albert earnestly. 'And I would love to show you the wonderful things I have found here and collected together.'

'No, dear Albert, I think I have suffered enough during the last few days from Victorian taste crystallized by the Almighty into the extraordinary scenery with which I have recently been surrounded. Not at all my period, dear. Corbusier, now—'

Here Sally gave the signal, as they say in books, for the ladies to leave the table, and presently took Mrs. Fairfax upstairs to powder her nose.

'You'll stay the night, of course?' she said.

'Alas! no, my dear. Very sweet of you, but we've taken rooms at Gleneagles for to-night. I really must push on. I should like to reach London, if possible, to-morrow, as my husband is passing through for one day on his way to America and I want to see him about being divorced, you know.'

Sally's murmured sympathy was waved aside.

146

'It's not been too successful, really—our marriage, I mean. I'm getting rather old for all the fuss and worry of having a husband, that's the truth. And how's yours getting on, my dear: still happy, are you? Has Walter settled down at all? I know you were rather worried about him at one time.'

'We're divinely happy,' said Sally, 'and it's wonderful being here. He hasn't a chance to spend money and he's been working harder than I've ever known him. You know, people are too hard on Walter. Of course he gives the impression of being all over the place, but that's only because of his high spirits. And then, poor darling, he has *no* idea of the value of money, which is sometimes very annoying for me as I'm by nature rather stingy.'

'I've hardly ever met a man who has any idea of the value of money,' said Mrs. Fairfax. 'It's one of the nice things about them. Now, women are nearly always mercenary creatures.'

'Oh! And, by the way, of course, I'd quite forgotten it—I'm going to have a baby.'

'Are you, Sally? Well, it does happen. Torture, my dear, but one looks lovely afterwards, which is a great consolation. I've had three, you know, and they all cut each other dead now; but they're devoted to me, specially dear Bellingham. By the way, I'm told that Potts (my second husband) has taken a house near here—Castle Bane. Dreary creature, Potts, but Héloïse is a dream. She's at the Lido now. I'm going out there really to see her. How lovely Jane was looking at dinner.

'Yes, wasn't she? It's a great secret, so don't say I told you, but she's engaged to Albert.'

'My dear, you amaze me! Will that be a success?'

147

'I really don't know. They are very much in love at present; but Jane is terribly sensitive, and Albert so much wrapped up in his work that I can't help feeling there will be trouble. So long as she understands 'his temperament—but I'm not sure how much she does. However, even if they're happy for a year or two it's more than lots of people get out of life.'

'Yes, you're perfectly right. I've lived through it and I know. I had two years of complete happiness with Cosmo, and about eighteen months with Campo Santo, and I can tell you that it makes all the rest of one's life worth while. But I don't really advise too much chopping and changing for most people: gets one into such restless habits. I couldn't have stayed with Cosmo after . . . Well, never mind. So I thought if I can't be happy I might as well be rich, and made off with Potts. Then, of course, I was bowled over by Campo Santo in ten minutes. Well, I always think that would have lasted, only the angel died on me quite suddenly: and there he was—Campo Santo in good earnest. It was dreadfully depressing. Still, there was little Bobs to cheer me up: quite the nicest of my children. Have you seen him? He's still at Eton, the precious. He's meeting me in Venice, too, when Héloïse leaves. They can't endure each other. Not frightened about this baby, are you?'

'Well, no, not really.'

'You needn't be; nobody dies in childbirth now, my dear. It's considered quite *vieux jeu*. And it may be a consolation to you to hear that the medical profession makes an almost invariable rule of saving the mother's life in preference to that of the child if there's any doubt about it. Sick much?'

148

'Yes, a whole lot.'

'Excellent! A very good sign. Now can we go and collect Ralph? I think we should soon be making off.'

They found the others standing round the drawing-room fire, the 'grown-ups' having taken themselves off to the study to hear a talk on Timbuctoo. Walter had happened to be passing the door when it began, and declared that the opening words, delivered by the evidently nervous speaker in a sort of screech, had been;

'PEOPLE who take their holidays abroad seldom think of Timbuctoo...'

'Very seldom, I should imagine,' said Albert. 'Loudie dear, I wonder if you would sing us this little song which I found in an album here? The words are by Selina Lady Craigdalloch (the genius who collected in this house so many art treasures), and the music is "By my dear friend, Lord Frances Watt." It has been my greatest wish to hear it sung by somebody ever since I found it.'

'I have often noticed,' said Ralph languidly, 'that all accompaniments between the years 1850 and 1890 were invariably written by the younger sons of dukes and marquesses. They seem to have had the monopoly—most peculiar.'

'I should love to sing it,' said Mrs. Fairfax, settling herself at the piano, 'and then we must go. Where is it—here? Oh, yes...'

To Bxxxxxxxxxxx
———

(Morte Poitrinaire)

She began to sing in a small, pretty voice:

149

When my dying eye is closing,
And my heart doth cease to beat;
Know that I in peace reposing,
Have but one, but one regret!

Leaving you, my only treasure,
Bitter is, and hard to bear,
For my love can know no measure;
Say then, say for me a prayer!

Lilies, darling, on me scatter,
And forget-me-nots, so blue;
What can this short parting matter?
We shall surely meet anew!

We shall meet where pain and sorrow,
Never more assail the breast;
Where there is nor night nor morrow
To disturb our endless rest.

'Beautiful!' cried Albert. 'And beautifully sung!'
'Well,' said Mrs. Fairfax, 'a very pretty little song. You know, Ralph dear, I think that we shall *have* to be going. Unfortunately we are still in the realm of night and morrow, and if we don't push on to Gleneagles we shall get no rest at all.'

There was a perfect chorus of dismay, but Mrs. Fairfax was adamant.

'Your figure is a dream, Ralph!' said Albert, as they followed her into the hall. 'Are you on a diet?'

'Yes, dear, most depressing. I got muscles from dancing too much, they turned into fat—*et voilà!* . . .'

'Do muscles turn into fat?'

'Of course they do. Haven't you noticed that all athletes become immense in their old age?'

'But this is very serious!' cried Albert, in a voice of horror. 'It should be brought to the notice of public schoolmasters. I myself shall give up walking and buy a little car. I sometimes walk quite a distance in Paris.'

'Nothing,' said Ralph mournfully, 'develops the muscles so much as driving. Good-bye, Albert. I hope to see you in London, dear.'

CHAPTER SIXTEEN

That night Jane found herself unable to go to sleep. Her brain was in a particularly lively condition and she tossed and turned thinking first of one thing and then of another until she felt she would go mad. 'Albert! Albert! Albert!' was the refrain.

'Shall I be happy with him in Paris? Will he be the same after we're married? Shall I interfere with his work? That, never,' she thought; 'I am far more ambitious even than he is and will help him in every possible way to achieve fame.

'If I lie quite still and breathe deeply I might manage to drop off to sleep. What shall I put on to-morrow? Not that jumper suit again. I wasn't looking so pretty to-day. I shan't look pretty to-morrow if I have no sleep. Perhaps if I get out of bed and walk up and down . . . Yes, now I'm feeling quite drowsy. I must write to mamma to-morrow, I haven't written for over a week. What shall I tell her? Oh, yes! the games would amuse her.'

Jane began to compose a letter in her head and was soon even more wide-awake than before. She had hardly ever in her life experienced any difficulty in going to sleep and it made her furious.

'I'll stay in bed till lunch-time to-morrow to make up for this,' she thought.

After about two hours of painful wakefulness she at last fell asleep, soothed, as it were, by a delicious smell of burning which was floating in at her bedroom window and of which she was only half conscious.

Hardly, it seemed to her, had she been dozing for five minutes when she was suddenly awakened by a tremendous banging on her door, which opened a moment afterwards. The electric light blazed into her eyes as she was struggling to open them.

'What is it?' she said, very angry at being awakened in this abrupt manner when she had only just gone to sleep with so much difficulty.

The butler was standing just inside the room.

'House on fire, miss. Will you please come downstairs immediately?'

Jane sat up in bed and collected her wits about her.

'Have I time to dress?' she asked.

'No, I think not, miss; the flames are spreading very rapidly to this part of the house, and Mr. Buggins wants everyone in the hall at once; he is holding a roll-call there.'

Jane leapt out of bed, put on some shoes and a coat, and taking her jewel-case from the dressing-table she ran along to Albert's room. She noticed that it was just after five o'clock.

The butler was still talking to Walter as she passed and Albert had not yet been awakened. Jane

152

put on the light and looked at him for a moment as he lay asleep, his head on one arm, his hair in his eyes.

'How beautiful he is,' she thought as she shook him by the shoulder.

'Wake up, darling, quick! The house is on fire. We've no time even to dress; so come with me now to the hall.'

Albert stretched and got out of bed. He was wide awake and perfectly calm.

'Go back to your room,' he said, 'and throw your clothes out of the window, or you'll have nothing to go home in. I'll do the same and come along for you when I've finished.'

'What a brilliant idea!'

Jane flew back to her room and in a very short time had thrown all her possessions on to the gravel outside. Presently Albert came running down the passage and they went, hand in hand, to join the others in the hall.

'Here they are! That's everybody, then.'

Mr. Buggins was cool and collected; it seemed perfectly natural that he, and not General Murgatroyd, should be taking charge of everything.

'Now,' he said in a firm voice. 'This part of the house is quite safe for the present, so as we are all here I think we might begin to save what we can.

'I must beg you all not to go upstairs again. The wing in which your bedrooms are situated is in a very dangerous position and will be the next to go. The dining-room must also, of course, be left to its fate, but we can safely collect things from the drawing-room, billiard- and smoking-rooms. I telephoned some time ago for the fire brigade, but I'm afraid it will be at least an hour before they can possibly arrive. When they come they will naturally decide for themselves where they can go; we *must* be on the safe side. The servants are all engaged with a chain of buckets in trying to prevent the garages and outhouses from catching, in which I think they may succeed. It would be useless for amateurs to attempt saving the house, the fire has much too firm a hold.'

The party dispersed into the various sitting-rooms leading out of the hall and began to work with a will.

Albert, at great personal danger, put a damp handkerchief over his mouth and dashed into the dining-room which was dense with smoke. Cutting them out of their frames with some difficulty he managed to save the portraits by Winterhalter of Selina, Lady Craigdalloch and her husband, the fourth Earl.

(The present Lady Craigdalloch was never able to forgive him this when she heard about it afterwards. It became her pet grievance.

'The dining-room,' she would say, 'was full of beautiful Raeburns, and what must the young idiot do but risk his life to save the two ugliest pictures in the house. It drives me mad.')

As he ran out of the castle to bestow the Winterhalters in a place of safety, Albert was amused to observe General Murgatroyd carrying with great care an enormous coloured print which had hung in the place of honour over the smoking-room mantelpiece. It was entitled 'The Grandest View in Europe,' thus leading one to expect a view of Mont Blanc, the Doge's Palace, Chartres Cathedral or some such popular beauty-spot, instead of which it depicted the back

154

of a horse's head as it would appear to the rider, with two large grey ears sticking up in the immediate foreground. Beyond the ears could be seen a stone wall which was being negotiated with success by two horses and with no success at all by a third. Hounds running across an adjacent field gave the clue to the whole thing; a hunt was evidently in progress. 'The Grandest View in Europe' having been reverently deposited among the rapidly growing collection of objects on the lawn, its saviour trotted back to the house, bent upon rescuing the head of a moose which hung in the hall.

Admiral Wenceslaus now staggered forth with a load of miscellaneous objects, including a chronometer, a model of the *Victory* in silver, a book entitled *The Triumph of Unarmed Forces*, which he had been trying for some time to lend to various members of the party, and several whisky bottles. Mr Buggins followed him with Prince Charlie's boot, several old family miniatures and a lock of Bothwell's hair.

Sally, looking rather green, sat tucked up on a sofa and watched these proceedings with some amusement. Albert stopped for a moment to ask her how she felt.

'Oh, quite all right, longing to help, but Walter made me promise I'd stay here.'

'D'you know how the fire started?'

'No; Haddock, the butler, says he has no idea at all. He discovered it, you know. The smoke was pouring in at his window and he says he only got some of the maids out just in time.'

When Albert went back to the house he noticed that flames were already beginning to envelop his own bedroom. Meeting Jane in the hall he kissed her hurriedly and said, 'Take care of yourself, my precious, won't you?' She was carrying the Jacob's Ladder.

He then saved his portrait of Sally and several albums containing water-colours from the billiard-room. Lady Prague was busy showing two men how to take the billiard-table to pieces. They had been managing far better before she came along.

Albert and Jane made many journeys and succeeded in saving all the plush chairs, bead stools, straw boxes, wax flowers, shell photograph-frames and other nineteenth-century objects which they had collected together from various parts of the house.

(When Lady Craigdalloch, far away in Africa, had recovered from the first shock of hearing that Dalloch Castle was razed to the ground, she said that, at any rate, all the Victorian rubbish there would now have vanished for ever and that this was a slight consolation. Her horror and amazement when, on her return, she was confronted by every scrap of that 'Victorian rubbish' which had always been such a thorn in her flesh, knew no bounds.)

At last all the furniture that it was possible to move reposed on the lawn in safety, and there was nothing left to do but sit 'like Lady Airlie in the ballad,' as Mr. Buggins remarked, and watch the house burn down.

A ghastly early morning light illuminated the faces of Lord Craigdalloch's unfortunate guests as they sat surrounded by the salvage from his home, which looked like nothing so much as the remains

156

of an auction sale before the buyers have moved their purchases.

> *Lot 1*.—Fine old Jacobean oak table suitable for entrance hall. Two assegais and a wastepaper basket.
> *Lot 2*.—Bust of the younger Pitt. Large sofa upholstered in Heal Chintz. Gong of Benares brass-work.
> *Lot 3*.—Case of stuffed grouse in summer and winter plumage. Chippendale writing-table. Large print of Flora McDonald (etc., etc.).

Albert and Jane looked round with some amusement at the different varieties of bedroom attire displayed upon other members of the party. Sally looked lovely in crêpe-de-chine pyjamas, over which she wore a tweed coat lined with fur. Lady Prague was also wrapped in a tweed coat over a linen nightdress and a Shetland wool cardigan. She wore goloshes over her bedroom slippers. Lord Prague, who had collapsed into an armchair, was shivering in a Jaeger dressing-gown which had a sort of cape elaborately trimmed with pale blue braid, and the general stood near him in khaki pyjamas and a manly overcoat. The admiral wore a mackintosh. His bare, white and skinny legs sticking out from beneath it bore witness to the fact that Admiral Wenceslaus was a devotee of the old-fashioned, but convenient, nightshirt.

Albert went to the other side of the castle and picked up the clothes which he and Jane had thrown out of their bedroom windows. Jane and Sally, on seeing them, gave high cries of delight, and retiring behind an adjacent wardrobe they began to dress. Walter and Albert did likewise, and

157

Albert was also able to lend a jumper and a pair of grey flannel trousers to Mr. Buggins. Everybody else secretly wished that they had had sufficient forethought to throw some clothes out of the windows; the morning air was distinctly chilly.

'I've still two pairs of trousers left,' said Albert, holding in one hand the orange tartan ones he had worn upon the moor, and in the other his bright blue pair. 'Won't somebody wear them? General, can I tempt you? Lady Prague, come now! No?'

'Will you lend them to me, young man?'

'Admiral—but, of course, how very kind of you, and how lucky that I have the *matelot* ones. You will feel quite at home in them. Here is a real fisherman's jersey, too, why, you'll be thinking you are back on the dear old flagship—with "Yo! ho! ho! and a bottle of rum."'

The admiral, who seemed rather overwhelmed by the foregoing events, retired behind a zebraskin screen to put on the trousers. He stayed there for some time, and when he finally emerged, carried his eye in his hand. Creeping up behind Lady Prague, he suddenly thrust it into her face, yelling out:

'Peek-uck-bo!'

Lady Prague uttered a piercing scream and ran away as fast as the clinging draperies of her night-dress would allow until, tripping over her goloshes, she fell heavily on the gravel and grazed her knees rather badly. General Murgatroyd and Mr. Buggins assisted her to a chair. After this she became more acid than ever.

Meanwhile the admiral again withdrew behind his screen, where he was found much later by Mr. Buggins and Sally, fast asleep on the ground.

'Poor old boy,' said Sally kindly, 'it's been too

158

much for him.'

'Humph! I think I can guess what has been too much for him.' And Mr. Buggins produced from under the cast-off night-shirt three empty whisky bottles. 'Might as well leave him there,' he said. 'Got a head like a horse; he'll be all right soon.'

The whole castle was now enveloped in flames, which rose to almost double its height—a terrifying spcctacle. Even more alarming was the noise, a deafening roar like the sound of huge waterfalls, broken every now and then by the crash of falling masonry. Birds and bats, fascinated by the glare, were to be seen flying to their doom; and two huge beech trees which stood near the house were completely blackened.

The little party on the lawn sat in a dazed silence, overawed by the sight of this catastrophe.

When the firemen arrived they were far too late to save anything but some outhouses. Not to be deprived of their fun, however, they were soon playing the hose indiscriminately upon the huge flames, the beech trees and the general, who unobserved had strolled up towards the house in order to have a better view. Dripping wet and speechless with rage he rushed back to the others, and was obliged to swallow his pride and borrow Albert's tartan trousers and orange sweater. The sight of him thus attired was too much for Sally and Walter, who became perfectly hysterical with laughter which they were unable to control, and finally they had to go for a long walk in order to regain their composure.

'I wonder what the effect of all this will be on Morris-Minerva?' said Sally.

'Are you feeling all right, my own—'

'Yes, quite now, thank you, darling. Will the poor angel have red hair and a fiery nature as the result of it?'

When they got back to the others they found that quite a little crowd was collected on the lawn, constantly augmented by people from neighbouring villages, who straggled by twos and threes up the drive.

Those members of the house-party who were not clothed were beginning to feel rather self-conscious. The sight-seers all followed the same procedure. They stood for some time gazing at the fire, saying: 'Hoots!'—'Wisha!'—'Mon it's gran'! and other unintelligible phrases of the kind, after which they had a good look at the survivors, coming up quite close and breathing heavily. They then inspected the *lares* and *penates* on the lawn, piece by piece, admiring or criticizing. Having taken their time and seen everything of interest, they sat about the place in little scattered groups and ate.

'Oh! I'm so hungry,' said Sally, breaking a long silence.

The others agreed miserably. Although it was in fact only seven o'clock they all felt as though it must at least be luncheon time. It never occurred to any of them to wonder what the next step would be, but they felt instinctively that they must now see the thing through and wait there until the last beam had fallen.

Sally asked the butler, who was busy counting silver, whether any food had been saved, but he replied that both kitchen and larder had been in flames by the time that he had discovered the fire. Lord Craigdalloch's factor came and spoke to Sally. He was in his shirt-sleeves, having been hard at

160

work nearly from the beginning.

'Good morning, Mrs. Monteath. This is a very sad business, is it not? His lordship will be most terribly upset, I'm afraid.'

'Oh! it's too dreadful. Of course, one can hardly realize yet what it means, one is only so thankful that nobody was hurt. Is the house properly insured?'

'It is insured, but I doubt whether the policy will anything like cover the loss. And then, you see, for sentimental reasons it is such a terrible tragedy. We hoped at first to be able to save Lady Muscatel's tower, but we were too late. I think, if I may say so, that you all did wonders in rescuing so much furniture. I have sent to the home farm for waggons, it must be put in safety as soon as may be. I don't like the looks of all these people: I'm sure they would think nothing of removing a few souvenirs here and there.'

Soon after half-past eight the house was a blackened ruin and the fire practically over. Walter and Mr. Buggins were just discussing what they should do next, when a large old-fashioned Daimler drove up, and a middle-aged man in a very long kilt got out of it. Mr. Buggins greeted him warmly and introduced him as Sir Ronald McFea.

'Should McFea show the knee?' whispered Albert to Jane. 'You see, he doesn't show it at all. Isn't it too fascinating?'

'This is a fearful thing,' said Sir Ronald. 'A fearful thing. My gillie came in just now and said Dalloch Castle had been burnt to the ground, he said. I couldn't believe it—couldn't believe it. Well, there it is. Poor old Craig. It will be a most terrible blow for him when he hears it; shouldn't wonder if

161

it kills him—shouldn't wonder at all. He worshipped the place, every stick and stone of it. Poor old boy.

'Now, my wife says you must all come over to Castle Fea and have some breakfast. She says you must be simply starving so she's getting it ready.

'Dear, dear! It must have been a near thing, too, for hardly any of you to have saved your clothes even—and the general in fancy dress. Never mind, we shall be able to fix you up all right, I don't wonder. Hadn't you better come along now?'

Brightening somewhat at the prospect of breakfast, they accepted Sir Ronald's invitation with joy. Even the admiral stopped trying to put on Prince Charlie's boot, and staggered with the rest of them towards the Daimler, which seemed by some miracle to hold them all. Sally arranged with the factor and Haddock that the servants should be boarded out in neighbouring cottages for the present, and said that she would come back later and make plans for them.

Castle Fea, though a sufficiently welcome asylum to the dazed and hungry survivors of the fire, proved to be a perfect temple of gloom. It in no way resembled a castle, being a large square house with Gothic chimneys and a Greek portico, situated in the midst of a perfect tangle of fir trees, laurels and other evergreens which grew nearly up to its windows. Mr. Buggins pointed out the ruins of the ancient fortress upon an adjacent mound.

'I should think the McFea who built this house must have shown his knee quite often,' murmured Albert as they got out of the car.

The inside of the house was, if anything, more oppressive than the outside. It was a mass of

162

badly-stuffed animals, stained glass and imitation French and old oak furniture. The pictures were of a terrifying realism.

However, the breakfast to which the party now settled down in grateful silence was more than excellent, and Lady McFea, an ugly, dowdy, but thoroughly nice woman, tactfully refrained from asking questions about the fire until all the poached eggs and scones had been consumed. It was indeed a heavenly meal and, when it was over, the Dalloch Castle refugees felt more able to cope with their immediate future.

Sir Ronald and Lady McFea begged that any who would care to do so should stay on at Castle Fea for a few days. Walter and Sally, after a short consultation with Mr. Buggins, decided to accept this kind offer, feeling that it was more or less their duty to remain on the spot until they should hear from the Craigdallochs.

All the others, however, decided to leave by the four-thirty train for London that afternoon, and sleepers were ordered for them by telephone. These arrangements having been made, the McFeas took those who had lost their clothes upstairs, and fitted them out as best they could.

Albert and Jane found themselves alone in the drawing-room and kissed each other quite a lot. Presently Jane said in a gloomy voice:

'I suppose I shall have to go home now; what shall you do, darling?'

'Well, Mr. Buggins most angelically says I can stay with him in London for as long as I like, so I think I shall do that. But hadn't I better go and see your parents fairly soon? After all, I shall have to meet them sometime, shan't I? And then we can be

163

properly engaged if they approve of me. How far is it by train to Stow-on-the-Wold?'

'Oh, the beastly hole! don't mention it to me or I shall burst into tears. About two-and-a-half hours, I suppose. And you needn't think they'll approve of you, darling, because they're quite certain to kick you straight out of the house.'

'Anyhow, I can but try: if I'm kicked out we'll elope. It's perfectly simple. Then I think you'd better go straight home to-morrow and more or less prepare them, and I'll come down for lunch on Thursday. If they like me I'll stay the night, and if not we'll both go back to London together. Good plan?'

'Yes, very good, I think. Sweetest!'

The rest of that day was spent in wandering about rather gloomily in the grounds of Castle Fea, and they were all quite pleased when the time came for them to say good-bye to kind Sir Ronald and his wife. The Monteaths, terribly depressed at the prospect of many more such days, waved to them from under the Gothic portico until the car was out of sight.

*   *   *

Jane, Albert and Mr. Buggins dined together in the train that evening. At the opposite table Lord and Lady Prague, Admiral Wenceslaus and General Murgatroyd made a congenial foursome.

Albert was tired and in a very bad temper. Jane, who had never seen him like that before, felt miserable and rather resentful, but Mr. Buggins was in excellent spirits, and when they confirmed his suspicion that they were engaged he ordered a

164

bottle of champagne to celebrate the occasion. Albert insisted on reading a book between the courses which were very slow in coming.

'Albert, darling, please don't read. After all, I shan't be seeing you after to-morrow, I do think you might talk to me; besides, it's so rude.'

Albert took no notice but went on with his book, a very boring history of the Angevin kings. Mr. Buggins, seeing that he was really not himself, tactfully tried to draw Jane into conversation, but she could not leave Albert alone.

'Albert, do stop reading. Mr Buggins, *isn't* it rude and disgusting of him?'

Mr. Buggins felt like shaking them both, but went on quite calmly with his dinner.

'Albert, really I do think even if you must read between the courses, honestly you needn't read while you're eating. Oh, well, of course, if you prefer those beastly old Angevin kings to conversation that's one thing...'

At last she quite lost her temper, and snatching the book from him she threw it out of the window. Albert behaved extremely well about this, but none the less he was furious with Jane, who, in her turn, was completely miserable. They each felt that they had been stupid and childish, but rather less so than the other, and were both longing secretly to make it up.

'Isn't it a pity,' said Mr. Buggins, 'for two people with as much sense of humour as you have to behave like this?'

'Well, I may have a sense of humour, I hope I have,' said Albert, 'but I see nothing funny in throwing an expensive book away like that; and, as

165

we've paid the bill, we might as well go to our sleepers.'

'Here's my share for dinner,' said Jane, offering it to Albert, who had paid for the two of them.

'I don't want it.'

Mr. Buggins got up and left them alone at their table.

'Don't be so silly, Jane.'

'Well, I'm not going to be your kept woman, thank you.'

'Oh! really! I thought that was just what you did want to be.'

'Certainly not; I happened to be in love with you and offered to be your mistress. That's quite different.'

'Exactly the same.'

'Quite different. Of course, I should have earned my own living.'

'Oh! I see. May I ask how?'

'Well, I'm not sure.'

'Nor am I; not at all sure.'

'I suppose I could be a model.'

Albert had a sudden vision of the fastidious Jane posing to a lot of half-washed French art students and burst out laughing.

'Darling, how absurd you are.'

'Well, it was horrid of you to be so cross and *horrid* of you to read, wasn't it?'

'Yes, beastly. And horrid of you to throw my book out of the window, wasn't it?'

'Yes, quite.'

'Yes, *very*.'

'Yes, very, then. Look, we're the last people left, we'd better go.'

'Well, give me a kiss.'

'Not in front of that waiter.'

166

'He's not looking.'

'He's coming to turn us out. We really must go.'

As Jane rolled into her sleeper she just stayed awake for long enough to think luxuriously of the contrast between her journey to Scotland three weeks ago and her present one.

'I know now for certain,' she thought, 'that I've never been really happy before.'

CHAPTER SEVENTEEN

To Jane's amazement, real or pretended, her parents remained perfectly calm when she told them that she was engaged. The fact was that it had long been their greatest wish to see her married, and almost any respectable young man of reasonable fortune would have been received by them with open arms. When, the following day, Albert made his appearance, they took an immediate liking to him.

He, on his side, was very agreeably surprised. Even allowing for a good deal of exaggeration, Jane's account of her father and mother had been far from encouraging, and all the way down in the train he had been bracing himself up to meet a pair of cruel old lunatics who would probably attempt to murder him at sight. Instead of this he was greeted by two charming and good-looking people who were not, as far as he could judge, particularly put off by his appearance.

Jane took him for a little walk in the garden before lunch. 'I told them all about it,' she said, 'and they weren't nearly so horrified as I thought they would be, but I dare say they think it's a cleverer plan to pretend not to mind at first. Apparently mamma used to know your mother quite well when they were girls. She says she was a great beauty.'

'Yes, she was very beautiful.'

'But they don't know yet that you're an artist. I expect that will upset them, all right.'

'Really, darling! To hear you talk one would think you wanted them to be upset. I believe you've got a totally wrong idea of your parents, you know. I've only had a glimpse of them so far, it's true, but they seem very nice and kind—quite different from what you led me to expect.'

'Oh, well, I suppose now you're going to take their side,' said Jane pettishly. 'Anyway, there's the bell for lunch, so come along. Perhaps you'll see my point when you know them better.'

During luncheon Albert realized that, as he had always been inclined to suspect, Jane's pretended hatred of her parents was the purest affectation. She was evidently very fond of them as they were of her. He thought it a curious anomaly that a person with such a straight-forward nature as Jane seemed to him to possess should be capable of deceiving herself to this extent upon any subject, but consoled himself by thinking that marriage would bring home the real truth to her.

The Dacres did not in any way show that they knew of Jane's engagement, but behaved to Albert quite as they would have to any other visitor. They were anxious to hear every little detail of the Dalloch house-party and laughed heartily at Albert's description of Lady Prague.

Encouraged by this he broached the subject of

168

General Murgatroyd, delicately, as he imagined from what Jane had said that no officer in the British Army would be considered a fit subject for jest. Great, therefore, was his amazement when Sir Hubert Dacre cried out:

'Not really! Was Mildew Murgatroyd there? Jane, you never told me that! Well, I'm sure you got plenty of fun out of him, didn't you?'

'What did you call him, sir?' asked Albert, hardly able to believe his ears.

'Mildew Murgatroyd. They called him that in the South African War because he was so untidy and slovenly. People used to say that even his revolver was coated with mildew. Why, he's a perfect joke in the army, you know. During the last War they wouldn't have him in France at all. He was given some job in connexion with the Inland Water Transport, I believe.'

'Oh *good*!' said Albert; 'only I wish I'd known it before. I pictured him leading his men like anything, from the way he talked. He told us a most blood-curdling story about how he and twenty privates held a kopje in South Africa, alone and unaided for a fortnight.'

'Yes, and did he tell you that when the relieving force came up in answer to his urgent messages they found there wasn't a Boer for thirty miles, hadn't been the whole time, you know, except in his own imagination.'

'Oh, why didn't we know all this before!' sighed Albert.

'I hear Buggins was up there,' went on Sir Hubert. 'Such a very nice, cultivated man, and a great authority on Scottish history.'

There was a silence. Albert began to feel very

169

much embarrassed; the end of the meal approached rapidly and he dreaded the moment when he would be left alone with Jane's father. He looked helplessly round the room for something to talk about, and presently said:

'What a lovely Richmond that is, Sir Hubert!'

'Yes, quite a pleasant picture in its way, I think. Those two children are boys, though with their long hair and frilly skirts one would rather suppose them to be girls. The one on the left is my father.'

'I see that it is painted in his earlier manner. I am inclined myself to prefer his middle period. Did Jane tell you that I was fortunate enough to be able to save two very beautiful pictures from the fire at Dalloch? Winterhalters. Is he a favourite of yours?'

'How funny,' said Lady Dacre, 'that it should be the fashion to admire those Victorian artists again after so many years.'

Albert, who rather particularly prided himself on being quite uninfluenced by such things as fashions, looked down his nose at this remark.

Lady Dacre now rose to her feet and Albert, with a sinking feeling in the pit of his stomach, was left alone with his future father-in-law.

He thought, 'Better get it over quickly,' and was beginning a beautiful and well-constructed sentence which he had made up in the train, when Sir Hubert interrupted him with:

'Have some more port?'

'Thank you, sir. The thing is,' Albert said hurriedly, forgetting all the rolling periods which he had been about to pour forth, 'Jane and I think . . . that is, we know . . . that we would like to get married.'

'Be married,' said Sir Hubert severely. 'I very

170

much dislike the expression "to get married."'

'So do I,' replied Albert earnestly.

'Then why use it? Well, so you and Jane wish to be married, do you? And isn't this a little sudden?'

'Sudden, sir?'

'How long have you known each other?'

'Oh, for a very long time—quite six weeks altogether, and we've been engaged for nearly a fortnight.'

'Yes, I see—a perfect lifetime! And have you the means to support her?'

'I have a thousand a year, beside what I can make.'

'And what is your profession?'

Albert felt his nerve vanishing.

'If I say "artist" he will kick me out of the house. I can't face it. I shall have to tell a lie.'

'I am in business, sir.'

'What business?'

'In the city.'

'Yes; but what is your business in the city?'

'Oh, I see! Yes, I'm a pawnbroker—did I say pawnbroker? I mean, stockbroker, of course.'

Sir Hubert looked deeply disgusted.

'I'm sorry to hear that,' he said, 'although in these days people must take what work they can get. I have always felt myself—no doubt wrongly—that stockbroking is a very unproductive sort of profession. If I had a son I should have wished him to choose almost any other, and I always imagined that Jane would end by marrying a man of talent, say, a writer or an artist. However, that's neither here no there, and I don't see that there can be much objection to your engagement. Jane is of an age to know her own mind. Personally,

I should advise you to wait for a few weeks before announcing it. Let's go to the drawing-room, if you've quite finished your port.'

Albert now wished that the earth would open up and swallow him. He also felt quite furious with Jane; and as soon as they were left alone together he fell upon her, tooth and nail.

'You little idiot! We can never be married now, and it's all your fault. I can't face your father again. I must go away this instant.'

'Albert darling, what d'you mean? Was he awful to you?'

'No, he was charming; but *why* did you say he hated artists?'

'Because I'm sure he does. It's the sort of thing he always hates.'

Albert told her what had happened.

'You see,' he cried miserably, 'it's impossible for me to stay here after that!'

Jane burst into fits of laughter. She laughed and laughed. Then, she kissed Albert on the tip of his nose and ran out of the room. Presently she returned with both her parents, who were laughing so much that the tears ran down their cheeks.

*   *   *

The Dacres were frankly delighted at Jane's engagement. It would hardly be fair to say that they were anxious to get her off their hands, but, fond as they were of her, there was no doubt that she had lately caused them an unending amount of worry. Her constant and violent flirtations with the most curiously unsuitable people, her doubtful friends, wild behaviour and increasingly bad reputation, all

172

these things were driving them demented, and they both felt that the only hope of steadying her lay in a happy marriage.

'I think we are very lucky,' said Sir Hubert, talking it over with his wife that night in bed. 'When you think what some of Jane's friends are like! Suppose, for instance, it had been Ralph Callendar, not very probable, I admit, but one never knows. Now this boy is of good family, has nice manners, was at Eton and all that, and at the same time he is intelligent. Jane could never have been happy with a fool. If he is a trifle affected—well, I don't know that that's such a terrible fault in a young man. Tiresome, of course, but pardonable. Altogether it seems to me quite satisfactory, far more so than I should ever have expected.'

The engagement was announced in the papers a few days later and as at that particular moment there happened to be a scarcity of news, Albert and Jane for one day vied with the Sudbury Murder Trial in holding the attention of the public.

'ROMANCE OF YOUNG ARTIST AND BARONET'S DAUGHTER.

SEQUEL TO FIRE AT DALLOCH CASTLE'

blared forth on the front page of the *Daily Runner* in type only a shade smaller and less black than that used for:

'*Tragic Widow's Eight-Hour Ordeal in Dock.*'

The gossip-writers, who have little or no use for tragic widows unless they are titled as well, gave the couple their individed attention.

Jane was described as tall and beautiful with artistic tastes, and was credited with having designed her own bedroom at her father's house in Wilton Crescent. (In point of fact, the bedroom had not been redecorated since they bought the house.)

Much capital was made out of the fact that they had both been staying at Dalloch Castle, the beautiful and historic seat of the Earl of Craigdalloch, when it was so tragically and mysteriously burnt to the ground.

'I hear, by the way,' said one paragraph, 'that Lord and Lady Craigdalloch (she, of course, was a daughter of the late Sir Robert Barns) are shortly returning to Scotland to superintend the rebuilding of the castle. As Lady Craigdalloch is renowned for her exquisite taste, the new castle will probably be an immense improvement on the old, which was built in 1860, a bad year—as some wit is said to have remarked—for wine, women and houses.'

Albert shuddered when he read this.

'My dear Jane, I can absolutely *see* the house that she will build. It is too horrible to think of that heavenly place gone for ever, but even more horrible to imagine, rising out of its ashes, a building in the best cenotaph style. I really believe that Lady Craigdalloch would pull down the Albert Memorial if she had a chance.'

Jane received, among others, the following letters of congratulations:

'DEAR JANE,
'Many congratulations on your engagement. I admit that it was a great surprise to me when I read it in *The Times* this morning.
'My husband has been far from well since the fire. He sends good wishes.

'Yrs. sincerely,
'FLORENCE PRAGUE.'

'She doesn't seem wildly enthusiastic,' said Albert, who read this over Jane's shoulder, 'but I rather think she was in love with me herself,' he added complacently.

'Marlborough Club.
'DEAR MISS DACRE,
'Congratulations.
'I caught a nasty chill after the fire so please excuse this short note.

'Yrs.,
MOWBRAY MURGATROYD.'

'Bachelors' Club.

'DEAR MISS DACRE,
'Hearty congratulations. After all we went through together I shall always remember you with great affection.
'What a gallant deed of yr. fiancé, saving those Winterhalters. I did not know of it until afterwards.

'Yrs. sincerely,
'STANISLAS WENCESLAUS.'

175

'Castle Fea.

'DARLING JANE,

'I'm *so* glad everything has passed off all right. I was certain your parents would like Albert myself, but I know that it was an anxiety to you, feeling that they might not approve. The McFeas have been angelic to us. We leave here to-morrow as everything seems to be fixed up now. What d'you think we found yesterday among the ruins of Dalloch? The admiral's spare eye. It was hollow inside and veiny, and I can't tell you what a really nasty look it gave us! Walter insists on wearing it hanging from his watch-chain, which is so disgusting of him.

'It's too awful all our things being burnt: as Walter says, it would have been cheaper in the end to go to the Lido. Still, if we had you'd never have met Albert, so it's all to the good, really.

'Morris-Minerva is making my life sheer hell at the moment. I throw up quite constantly.

'Best love. Come and see us soon.

'SALLY.'

Poor Jane found that it took her the best part of that day to answer these—and some thirty-five other letters, and Albert felt himself rather neglected. When the next morning she received not thirty-five but sixty-five, he announced that he would go to Paris until this influx of congratulations was over.

'But my dear,' said Lady Dacre, 'when the letters come to an end the presents will begin, and that is much worse, because it is such an effort pretending to be grateful for absolute horrors.

176

'Hubert and I were discussing your plans this morning, and we think that if you want to be married in November we had better go back quite soon to Wilton Crescent. There is Jane's trousseau to be ordered, for one thing.'

'If you do that I can stay with Mr. Buggins, but meanwhile I really think I had better go over to Paris for a bit. I ought to be getting rid of my present studio, and have several things that must be seen to sometime soon. I won't bother to look for a new flat yet. We can stay in an hotel after our honeymoon, until we find a nice one, but I must wind up my affairs, and this seems to be a good moment. Jane is far too much occupied to need me about the place now.'

CHAPTER EIGHTEEN

Albert went to Paris meaning to stay there for a fortnight, but in a week's time he was standing outside the Dacres' front door in Wilton Crescent. Frankly, he had not enjoyed himself and had spent his time counting the hours to when he should see Jane again. This worried him a great deal. Always before he had been perfectly happy in Paris and he had expected to be so still—had thought that he would hardly miss her at all and that he might even find it quite an effort to come back to her, instead of which he found himself restless and miserable and unable to stay away. He began to realize that nothing would ever again be as it had been for him, and the realization annoyed him.

He found Jane alone in the downstairs

177

drawing-room; she was not expecting him and flew into his arms.

'Darling sweetest,' she said after a few minutes, 'don't go away again. It was dreadful, I had to be thinking about you the whole time.'

'I got so bored with thinking about you that I had to come back.'

'Angel, did you really? I am pleased. Come and see the presents, they're simply unbelievable!' And she dragged him upstairs to a large empty room which had been set aside for the wedding presents.

'There are masses for you, too. I put them all over there. Shall we unpack them now?'

'Let's look at yours first. My dear, what a lot, though! You must know a quantity of people. But how absolutely horrible they are! What on earth shall we do with all these atrocious things? And where do people go to buy wedding presents? Is there a special shop for them, because these things are all exactly alike? Have you noticed that? Oh, look at the Lalique, and all that dreadful glass with bubbles in it! I shall burst into tears in a moment.'

'Oh, well,' said Jane, 'don't take it to heart too much. It only needs a good kick.'

'I know what we'll do,' said Albert, 'we'll have a wedding-present shoot, and get General Murgatroyd to arrange it for us. You see, the drivers can throw the things over our heads and we'll shoot at them. Then, when it's all over, we'll be photographed with the bag. Haven't you any nice presents, darling?'

'Not one,' said Jane, sadly. 'Now let's open yours.'

They set to work, and soon the floor was covered with brown paper, shavings and pieces of string.

Whereas Jane's presents were nearly all made of glass, Albert's seemed to consist mainly of leatherwork. Leather blotters, waste-paper baskets and note-cases were unpacked in quick succession, and lastly, a cigarette box made out of an old book. This present, which was sent by someone he had known at Oxford, perfectly enraged Albert: it had originally contained the works of Mrs. Hemans.

'My favourite poetess. Why couldn't he send me the book unmutilated? He must remember that I never smoke, in any case. Still, sweet of him to think of me.'

The maid came in with some more parcels for Jane, containing a Lalique clock from Lady Brenda. ('How kind! considering we've only met her once. It will do for the shoot, too.') A lampshade made out of somebody's last will and testament, and a hideous little glass tree, growing in a china pot, from Lady Prague.

'I'm beginning to understand about wedding presents,' said Albert. 'It seems to me that they can be divided into three categories: the would-be useful, the so-called ornamental, and those that have been converted from their original purpose into something quite different, but which is seldom either useful or ornamental.'

'I think,' said Jane bitterly, 'that they can be divided into two categories: those that have been bought in a shop, which are beastly, and those that have been snatched off the mantelpiece and given to the butler to pack up, which are beastlier. Look here, Albert darling, I'm getting really sick of this wedding. I do nothing all day but thank for these revolting presents, which I would pay anybody to take away, and try on clothes I don't want. Couldn't we chuck the whole thing and be married quietly somewhere? If I have to face another two months like this I shall be ill. Really, I mean it. Please, Albert.'

'Well, darling, personally, I think it would be heaven, but I must be in London for my exhibition, you know.'

'When does that open?'

'In three weeks to-morrow.'

'That gives us heaps of time to have a honeymoon and everything. Please, let's do that. Go and see about a special licence, now, this minute.'

'But, darling, listen to me...'

'Oh, well, if you are going to be tiresome...'

'Very well, I'll see what can be done, but first we must ask your parents. No, I absolutely insist on that, darling.'

Sir Hubert and Lady Dacre, as might have been expected, showed no enthusiasm at all when told of Jane's little plan.

'Don't be stupid,' said Lady Dacre scornfully, 'of course you can't do any such thing. People would say at once that Jane is going to have a baby. The presents will get better soon, I dare say: probably you won't have a great many more, and anyhow, the nicest ones generally come at the end.'

'Why not advance the date a little,' suggested Sir Hubert, 'to, say, the middle of October, about a month from now? That would be much more sensible than rushing off in such a hurry, and after all, a month does go fairly quickly.'

Jane and Albert felt the justice of these remarks and decided that they would definitely settle on the sixteenth of October, by which time Albert's exhibition would be well begun.

180

'If only,' said Jane, 'when announcing a marriage, one could put, "No presents, by request," how much more bearable the life of engaged couples would become. Look what I've got to thank for now. A pair of bellows made from the timbers of the *Victory* and sent by Admiral Wenceslaus. Oh, dear!'

'Very kind of him, I think,' said her father reprovingly.

'Oh, well; yes, so it is. Very kind of all the people who send these inferior things. I only wish they wouldn't, that's all.'

'How much better it would be,' sighed Lady Dacre, 'if *everybody* would send cheques.'

'Or postal orders,' said Jane.

'Or stamps,' said Albert.

For the next week or two, Jane and Albert had to make up their minds that they would only see each other once a day. They generally dined together and sometimes went to a play, but were often too tired even for that. Presents poured in for both of them, over and above which Albert was now very busy arranging about his exhibition.

He found that he had not brought over quite enough pictures for it, and embarked on a series of woolwork designs for six chairs, based on the theme of sport in the Highlands. He also completed his 'Catalogue of Recent Finds at Dalloch' (having wired for and obtained the consent of the Craigdallochs), intending that a specimen copy should be on view at the exhibition.

With Albert thus kept so busy that anyhow he would have had no time to play with her, Jane found her own jobs far less disagreeable. As Lady Dacre had predicted, the presents she received greatly improved in quality as time went on and she found it much less boring to write letters thanking for things that she really liked. Her trousseau now became a source of great interest, especially the wedding dress, which she could not try on often enough and which was extremely lovely. As for the other things, tiring as it undoubtedly was to stand for hours every day being fitted, there was a certain excitement about the idea that by the time she began to wear them she would be a married woman, and this sustained her.

CHAPTER NINETEEN

Walter and Sally Monteath, on their return to London, found themselves financially in a very bad way indeed. They had lost almost all their personal effects in the fire. Although they replaced these as economically as they could, it took most of their available money to do so. At this inconvenient moment the accumulated bills of months began to rain upon them, more numerous and insistent than ever before. The bank refused to allow them a further overdraft, all Sally's jewellery had long since been sold, and she began to have difficulty even in paying the household books.

Sally felt desperately ill and worried, and even Walter was obliged to give up taking taxis everywhere; but, apart from that, the situation did not appear to weigh on him at all until, one evening, he came in with some books that he was going to review and found her crying bitterly.

'Sally, darling angel! What *is* the matter?' he

said, kneeling down beside her and stroking her hair. When, through her tears, she explained to him that she could bear it no longer, that she literally didn't know how to raise money for the week's books, and that she had been adding up what they owed and found it amounted to nearly a thousand pounds, Walter was enormously relieved.

'I thought something frightful must have happened,' he said. 'But if that's all you're worrying about, I can easily get some money. Why, anybody would lend us a hundred pounds or so to carry on with till our next quarter comes in. As for the bills, they can wait for years, if necessary.'

'Walter, they *can't*. Why, some of them have lawyer's letters with them already. And it's no use borrowing a hundred pounds—that won't really help us at all, permanently, I mean. Then think of Morris-Minerva. How expensive all that business will be, and how are we going to educate him, or anything?' She burst into fresh floods of tears and said wildly that she must have been mad to marry him on so little money but that she had thought they would be able to manage, and that so they would have, except for his idiotic extravagance.

Walter, who had never before in his life known Sally to utter a cross word, was amazed by this outburst and began to feel really worried. His was the sort of mentality which never apprehends an unpleasant situation until it is presented so forcibly that it can no longer be ignored. Now, for the first time, he began to see that their position was, in fact, very parlous, and he was plunged into extreme despair.

'Anyhow, darling,' he said, 'I can't have you worrying like this. Leave it all to me. I'll find a job and support you properly. I'll go out now, this minute, and find one,' he added, and seizing his hat he dashed out of the house, saying that he would come back when he had some work, and not before.

Sally felt strangely comforted by his attitude, although not very optimistic about the job. She sat by the fire and thought that, after all, these bothers were very trifling matters compared to the happiness of being married to Walter.

While she was sitting there thinking vaguely about him, there was a resounding peal on the front-door bell.

Sally remembered that the daily woman had gone home, and was half-considering whether she would sit still and pretend that everybody was out, when it occurred to her that it might be Walter, who was in the constant habit of losing his latch-key. The bell rang again, and this time Sally, almost mechanically, went to the door and opened it.

She was a little bit alarmed to see, standing in the passage, three tall bearded strangers, but was soon reassured by the unmistakably gloomy voice of Ralph Callendar which issued from behind one of the beards, and said:

'Sally, dear, I hadn't realized until this very moment that you are *enceinte*. How beautifully it suits you! Why had nobody told me?'

Sally laughed and led the way into the drawing-room. She now saw that the other men were Jasper Spengal and Julius Raynor, very efficiently disguised.

'Yes,' she said, 'but how *could* you tell? It's really very exciting, due in April. Morris, if a boy, Minerva, if a girl, and we haven't the slightest idea where she's going to live (there's no room here, as

184

you know) or how we can afford to educate him. But Walter's out now, looking for a job. Have a cocktail, Ralph dear, be an angel and make one; the things live in that chest. But why fancy dress so early in the evening, and why haven't we been asked to the party?'

'No, dear,' said Ralph sadly, taking some bottles out of the chest. 'Not fancy dress at all—disguise.'

'Are you—not wanted by Scotland Yard for anything, I hope?'

'No, dear, curiously enough. No; we are going, simply in order to please Jasper, to the Savoy Theatre, where we shall see a Gilbert and Sullivan operette, called—what is it called, Jasper?'

'"I Gondolieri."'

'Yes, "I Gondolieri." Jasper has a new philosophy, which is that one should experience everything pleasant and unpleasant, and says that nobody ought to die until they have seen one Gilbert and Sullivan operetta and one Barrie play. Last night he begged us to accompany him on these grim errands, and after much talk, we allowed ourselves to be persuaded. But as it would be impossible to explain this to all the casual acquaintances whom we might meet at the theatre, we decided to take the precaution of a disguise.

'It is one thing to see a Gilbert and Sullivan, and quite another to be seen at one. We have our unborn children to consider, not to mention our careers.

'It has taken us nearly all day, but I think the result satisfactory. To complete the illusion we intend to limp about during the *entr'acte*. Jasper, as you see, has a slight hump on one shoulder, and Julius a snub nose.

185

'I myself, have not been obliged to go to such lengths. Nobody would ever suspect me. Even if I went undisguised, they would only say, "We didn't know Ralph had a double." Did you mention, Sally, that Walter is looking for a job?'

'Yes, poor lamb, he is.'

'He won't find one, of course. But never mind, there are worse things than poverty, though I can't for the moment remember what they are, and we'll all take it in turns to keep the baby for you. A poet of Walter's ability has no business with money troubles and jobs and nonsense like that. Are you very hard up at the moment, Sally?'

'Yes, terribly, you know. We've got such debts and then our people simply can't help. They give us more than they can afford as it is.'

'Well, then, my dear, I'll tell you what to do, straight away. Come and live with me till Christmas and let the flat to an American woman I know for twenty guineas a week. Would that help?'

'Ralph, what an angel you are! But, of course, we can't do that, and we're not really so hard up, you know, only one likes a little grumble. Anyway, who would pay twenty guineas for a tiny flat like this? What are you doing?'

'Hullo! Regent 3146,' said Ralph into the telephone, his eyes on the ceiling. 'Hullo! Mrs. Swangard? Ralph here. Yes, I found you the very thing—a jewel, 65 Fitzroy Square. Belongs, you know, to the famous poet Monteath. Yes, I had the greatest difficulty . . . Oh, no, no trouble. I knew at once it would be *the* place for you. Heart of Bloomsbury . . . Oh, most fashionable, all the famous people . . . Yes, all round you, roaring away. What? I said "roaringly gay" . . . My dear, you'll be astounded when I tell you ... only twenty guineas! A *week*, not a day.

'Wonderful, yes. Of course, they wouldn't let it to just anybody, as you can imagine ... No ... As soon as you like—to-morrow if you like ... To-morrow, then ... Yes, I'll come round and see you about it after the play to-night ... Yes, perfect ... good-bye.'

'Oh, Ralph!' said Sally, almost in tears. 'How sweet you are! That means more than a hundred pounds, doesn't it, and almost at once? Think what a help it will be. That is, if she likes the flat; but perhaps she won't?'

'My dear, that woman will like just exactly what I tell her to like. So pack up and come round some time in the morning. There's a good-sized bedroom you can have, if you don't mind sharing my sitting-room. Oh, nonsense, darling, you'd do the same by me, as you know very well. The poor are always good to each other. Are you going to Albert's private view?' he added, as though anxious to change the subject.

'Oh, that's to-morrow, of course, I'd forgotten. Yes, we're supposed to be lunching with him first.'

'I hear he's given Jane for an engagement ring a garnet with Queen Victoria's head carved on it.'

'No! has he? Have you any idea at all what his pictures will be like?'

'Absolutely none; but Bennet, I believe, thinks well of them.'

Jasper and Julius, who had been looking at *Vogue*, now came over to the fireplace. Feeling that they had so far not quite earned their cocktails, they began to pour forth a flood of semi-brilliant conversation, mostly in Cockney, told two stories

187

about George Moore, one about Sir Thomas Beecham, asked if there was any future for Delius, and left, taking Ralph with them.

Sally resumed her meditations. How right she had been to marry Walter after all. Nobody could have made her so happy; life with him was very nearly perfect. The same tastes, the same friends, the same sense of humour and, above all, no jealousy. She dropped happily into an almost voluptuous doze. The rain was falling outside, which made the room seem particularly warm and comfortable.

Her thoughts became more and more misty, and chased each other through her head in the most inconsequent way until they were nonsense and she was on the edge of sleep—'When the rain is falling thickly there should be long white hands waving in it.'

Walter, finding her fast asleep on the floor, her head buried in a cushion, wondered whose were the empty cocktail glasses. He found a thimbleful of cocktail left in the shaker which he drank, and then woke up Sally by kissing her.

'It's no good, darling,' he said, 'I cannot dig, and to write gossip I'm ashamed, but I've borrowed ten pounds from Albert, and I love you dreadfully, and I'll write some articles for the Sunday papers. We'll get rich somehow. Meanwhile, I'm going to take you out to dinner at Quaglino's because you haven't been there and it might amuse you. And who's been drinking out of my cocktail glasses, I should like to know?'

'I made a hundred pounds while you were out, my angel, by letting the flat to an American friend of Ralph's from tomorrow, and Ralph says we can go and live in Gower Street while it's let; he's got a bedroom all ready for us. So what d'you think of that, sweetest?'

'Well, I think that beggars can't be choosers. If it's a load off your mind, I'm glad and, of course, it's divine of Ralph. Still, of course, really it's too bloody, because we shall never have a single minute to ourselves. You know what it is in Ralph's flat—one long party.'

'I know, darling, but it's only for six weeks, and it will be such a saving. Also, I didn't like to hurt his feelings by refusing, it was so sweet of him to think of it. As a matter of fact, we could go for some of the time to my family: they're always asking us to stay with them.'

'I believe it would be cheaper in the end,' said Walter crossly, 'to stay on here. Couldn't you telephone to Ralph and say that we've changed our minds?'

'No, darling, I couldn't. If you can't support me, somebody must, you know, and as we're both devoted to Ralph why not let it be he? We needn't really go to the family, of course; I only said that to annoy you, although I shall have to go sometime. By the way, too, remind me to tell mother about Morris-Minerva. I'm sure I ought to have told her ages ago, because it's the sort of thing it drives her mad to hear from somebody else.

'Darling Walter. And I'm sorry I said all that about supporting me, because I know you would like to be able to. And anyway, we're so much happier like this than if you had some horrid sort of job which you hated. And if we're really going to Quaglino's hadn't you better telephone for a table, my sweet?'

CHAPTER TWENTY

Albert had decided that the private view of his pictures should take the form of a giant cocktail-party at the Chelsea Galleries, where they were being exhibited, the afternoon before they were to be opened to the public. Guests were invited from half-past three to seven, and at three o'clock Albert and Jane, supported by the Monteaths and Mr. Buggins, with whom they had all been lunching, arrived at the Galleries in a state of some trepidation.

Walter and Sally, who had not seen the pictures before, gasped with amazement as they entered the room, and for several moments were left quite speechless. The pictures were indeed, at first sight, most peculiar and Albert appeared to have employed any medium but the usual. Some of them stood right out like bas reliefs, while various objects such as hair, beards, buttons and spectacles were stuck on to them. Others were executed entirely in string, newspaper and bits of coloured glass.

The first picture—*Child with Doll*—had a real doll stuck across it. The child also had real hair tied up with blue ribbons. The next on the catalogue, '*No 2; Fire irons, formal design*,' represented a poker and tongs and was executed in small pearl buttons, varying in shade from dead white to smoke-grey. This was framed in empty cotton-reels.

The most important picture in the exhibition was '*No. 15. The Absinthe Drinker.*' This was tremendously built out, the central figure—that of a woman—being in a very high relief. On her head was perched half a straw hat with black ostrich feathers. In one hand was a glass filled with *real* absinthe. This was felt by Albert himself to be his masterpiece.

The only painting in the ordinary sense of the word was his portrait of Sally, which, hung between two huge still-lifes with surgical limbs, stuffed birds and ukuleles stuck all over them, hardly showed up to its best advantage.

Mr. Buggins was rather shocked at this travesty of painting, but was nevertheless obliged to admit that there was a great deal of force in the pictures, while the Monteaths, when the first sensation of surprise had left them, pronounced themselves in raptures.

Albert was evidently in a state of nerves and hardly listened to what was said, but went from picture to picture, adjusting the feathers of *The Absinthe Drinker* at a slightly less-tipsy angle, retying one of *Child with Doll*'s hair-ribbons and borrowing Jane's comb with which to tidy its hair. Finally, he ran round combing all the hair and beards that he could find.

The others stood about rather gloomily wishing that the party would begin. Albert's nervousness had imparted itself to them and especially to Jane, who was terrified that the pictures (much as she personally admired them) might be a most dreadful failure.

If this happened, she thought selfishly, a gloom would certainly be cast over their whole wedding.

Albert, from having always before been perfectly indifferent as to what people might think of his work, now that the pictures were about to be exhibited had become almost childishly anxious for

191

them to have a success.

The first guest appeared in the shape of Ralph, who was received with exaggerated cries of joy.

'Ralph dear, how nice of you to come so early! We *were* hoping someone would come soon. You will try and make the party go, Ralph, won't you?' We're all simply terrified, and it's sure to be sticky at first, so promise to help?'

Ralph smiled sadly.

'So these are your pictures, Albert,' he said, and very slowly walked round the Gallery, carefully examining each one from various angles. Having completed the tour he went up to Albert and said earnestly, '*Go on* painting, Albert. I mean that. Go on with it and one day you will be a very considerable artist indeed. Good-bye, my dears, I must go home to bed.'

'Don't go!' they cried in disappointed voices; but he took no notice of their protestations and left the Gallery.

Albert wiped his eyes. He was more than touched and flattered by this attitude of Ralph's, and followed his friend out into the street to tell him so.

Jane broke rather an awkward silence by wondering who the next visitor would be. It was felt that Ralph had not exactly proved the life and soul of the party.

'I think this is quite awful,' said Walter. 'I'm not easily frightened myself, but the beginning of a party is always apt to upset me; and now in addition to the social fear I'm suffering, there is this enormous empty room with Albert's terrifying pictures. The whole atmosphere is painful to a degree. Not that I don't think the pictures very clever, mind you, Jane, because I do, and they will certainly cause a great sensation, but you must admit that they *are* terrifying, specially for that child. Sally, darling, I beg you won't look at it for too long, because if Morris-Minerva even faintly resembles it I shall commit infanticide on the spot.'

Sally now had a brainwave.

'Why don't we begin the cocktails?'

This brilliant idea was immediately acted upon, and when Albert came back a more cheerful atmosphere was pervading the whole place. He felt glad of a drink himself after an emotional scene with Ralph in the street.

The next arrival was Admiral Wenceslaus, who came in rather jauntily, saying:

'And don't offer me a cocktail; I never touch the things. How are you? How are you all?'

He took the cocktail which Albert was rather diffidently holding out towards him and drank it off at a single gulp.

'My dear Gates, I have brought back your trousers which I have had well pressed for you. They needed it. And also a little wedding present in the shape of a book which I thought you might read on your honeymoon. It is by an old friend of my own, Admiral Sir Bartelmass Jenks, and is entitled *The Prize Courts and Their Functions or The Truth About Blockade*. The prize courts, my dear Gates, as you know, investigate the case of ships captured in times of war . . .'

At this moment, as so often happens at parties, about twenty people all came in a lump together and the admiral, deprived of his audience, settled down to some more cocktails.

Soon the room was buzzing and humming with talk. The pictures, as Walter had foreseen, were

193

causing a real sensation. People were, for the most part, very guarded in their criticism, asking each other rather anxiously what they thought about them.

Not so, however, Lady Prague, who, imposing but dowdy in a coat of Paisley pattern with brown fur, was accompanied by General Murgatroyd and Lady Brenda Chadlington.

She walked round the Gallery rather flat-footedly, pausing here and there to inspect the more outstanding pictures rather closely with her nose almost touching them, and then at an exaggerated distance (a trick she had learnt while visiting the Royal Academy).

When she had completed this tour she turned to Lady Brenda.

'Of course, Brenda, I expect it's my own fault, but I really think these pictures are very ugly. Not the sort of thing I should care to have in a drawing-room at all. In fact, I don't see that you could call this Art. I mean, when you think of those wonderful Dutch pictures we saw last year. These are so terribly out of drawing. And then, all that hair! Well, I suppose they're very clever, but—'

Lady Brenda said, 'Ssh! they will hear you,' and General Murgatroyd said loudly and angrily that it was another art hoax and that he was not the least taken in by it.

'If you want to see some really good pictures,' he said, 'go to the Army and Navy Stores. There's one I saw yesterday—some sheep going into a little birch wood with a mist—early morning, I should say. I think of buying it for Craig's silver wedding—silver birches, you know; makes it rather suitable.'

'Personally, I'm glad I have a sense of humour,' went on Lady Prague, warming to her subject. 'That controversy about Rima now: what I said was, "Why be angry? Every time you want a good laugh in future you only have to go into Hyde Park and there it is!" Killing! A perfect scream!

'Ah! here's Jane. Well, my dear, congratulations on your engagement. We are just admiring your fiancé's pictures—quite pretty, aren't they? No cocktail, thank you, dear. I'm *not* very modern, I'm afraid.'

The Gallery was suddenly and surprisingly invaded by a large crowd of people dressed in the deepest mourning and carrying wreaths; among others, Jasper Spengal, who rushed up to Albert saying breathlessly:

'Such heaven, my dear! We've just been having a mock funeral. We bought a plot at the London Necropolis and we drove for miles and miles through the streets in carriages with black horses, and all the time Julius was in the coffin in grave-clothes which we bought at Harrods. And, did you know that one has grave-stockings, too? Then, when we reached our plot in the Necrop., he just pushed up the lid and walked out, and we all picked up the wreaths and ran for dear life.

'Oh, I wish you could have seen the gravediggers' faces! It was a really beautiful moment. Then we all packed into my car and Rosie's car and came on here, and we've brought the flowers for you and Jane because you are engaged. So suitable, we think,' and he laid his wreath at Albert's feet. An enormous card was tied to it, bearing the inscription:

'Sweets to the Sweet. In memory of a noble life.
R.I.P.'

Lady Prague, who had been drinking in every word of all this, said loudly and angrily, 'Those are the Bright Young People, no doubt. How very disgusting! Come along, Brenda, I'm going. Can I drop you anywhere, Mowbray?'

'Yes, if you happen to be passing the Marlborough . . .'

'Oh, darling!' cried Jasper. 'Did you hear what she called us? What a name! Bright Young People! Oh, how unkind to suggest that we are bright—horrid word—I see nothing bright about a funeral, anyway, do you? What a nasty old woman! I'm so—so glad she's gone!

'Now, darling, I must telephone—may I?—to the *Daily Runner* and tell them all about it: they'll just have nice time to write it up. We had six photographers and a cinematograph at the graveside, and the light has been very good to-day, luckily. Would you like to be photographed among the wreaths, darling? It might give quite a good boost to the exhibition.'

'I think not, Jasper, thank you so much. The Press people were here this morning and this is by way of being serious, you know, not a "freak party,"' said Albert rather crossly. His nerves were on edge, and the mock funeral, which would at any other time have amused him a lot, struck him as being a painfully stupid idea.

He was thankful when they all dashed away to hear the Will read at Jasper's house, leaving the wreaths piled up underneath *The Absinthe Drinker*, especially as Jane's father and mother came in a moment later.

The Dacres, of course, thought Albert's pictures perfectly raving mad, although they were too polite to say so. They had come with every intention of buying one, but decided in whispers that they were too dreadful—even for a lavatory, so they ordered copies of 'Recent Finds at Dalloch Castle' instead. While they were doing this, they noticed that Mrs. Fairfax had arrived, and Lady Dacre, remarking that she refused to shake hands with that woman, left the Gallery, with Sir Hubert in tow.

'My dear!' said Mrs. Fairfax to Albert, 'I had to come round for a moment to support you, but I am most frightfully busy. Have you heard the news? Well, I'm going to marry Cosmo again, which is lovely, because I do enjoy being a duchess when all's said and done, and now, with any luck, I shall be one for the rest of my life. You can't think what a difference it makes in shops and trains. Aren't your pictures divine? Especially the one of Florence in tweed.

'Ralph and I were furious to miss the fire, but it was lucky I went to Gleneagles, because that's where I met Cosmo again—in the swimmingbath— and we got on so well comparing notes about our various husbands and wives that we fixed it up there and then; so I must fly now and get on with my trousseau. If I have another baby, what relation will it be to Bellingham? Good-bye, darling, then. I really have to go.'

Isaac Manuel, the art critic and collector, now put in an appearance, and Albert spent nearly an hour going round the pictures with him. He was greatly soothed and comforted by the older man's intelligent appreciation of his work.

'You are very young,' he said to Albert as he was leaving, 'and your style is often crude and bombastic, but all the same, Mr. Gates, I must admit that I am very favourably impressed. I have not enjoyed an afternoon so much for some time. I predict a future for you if you realize, as I can see you do, that these methods are, in themselves, far from satisfactory and only a means to an end. Keep the end always in view and you may become a very good artist indeed. I shall certainly see that you have an excellent notice in my paper, and shall most probably present one of your pictures to the Nation. Good day.'

When Albert returned to the Gallery from seeing Mr. Manuel into the street, he found that everyone had gone except Jane, Sally, Walter and the admiral who appeared to have fallen asleep among the funeral wreaths, a terrifying sight as his glass eye remained open, fixed upon the ceiling in a fearful stare.

'What do you think that horrid old admiral has done?' cried Jane. 'To start with he drank so many cocktails that there weren't nearly enough to go round, and then when they were finished he got a straw from one of the wreaths and drank all the absinthe out of the glass in your picture. Sally actually saw him do it.'

'No, really that's too much,' said Albert, who couldn't help laughing all the same. 'I suppose in future I shall be obliged to fill that glass with coloured water, otherwise people will make a habit of drinking it, and you can see for yourselves how terribly the colour values are disturbed when the glass is empty.'

'Well, my dear Albert, I congratulate you,' said

Walter warmly. 'The whole thing was a great success, a really good party. And everyone thought the pictures quite brilliant. Manuel was very much impressed. I heard him tell Mr. Buggins that he intends to buy one for his collection, and most probably one for the Nation.'

'Clever Albert,' said Jane. 'Darling, I'm so pleased, aren't you? What's the time, by the way?'

'Past seven. We'd better go, I think. No one's likely to come now, and we'll have to be rather quick if we're really dining at eight.'

They picked up their bags, hats and other belongings and began to move towards the door, when Walter said:

'Look here! What about the admiral? He seems to have passed out completely among those lilies. We can't very well leave him like that, can we?'

Albert considered.

'No, I suppose we can't. Hadn't we better put him into a taxi and send him home? I expect we could carry him between us, Walter; or if he's too heavy I'll call the commissionaire to help.'

They advanced upon the admiral, Walter taking his shoulders and Albert his legs, and half-carried, half-dragged him to the street. Jane hailed a taxi into which they bundled him and shut the door.

'Where to, sir?'

'Oh! Walter, where does he live?'

'How should I know? I haven't an idea.'

'Well, where shall we send him?'

Silence.

'Wait a minute,' said Walter. 'Isn't there a special place somewhere for admirals? Now what *is* it called—Oh, yes! I remember, of course.'

He gave the taxi-driver half-a-crown and said:
'Take this gentleman to the Admiralty, please.'

CHAPTER TWENTY-ONE

The front page of next morning's *Daily Runner* was
full of interest to members of the recent house-party
at Dalloch Castle. Jane read it, as she always did,
while breakfasting in bed; and for once in her life
she pored over its columns with absolutely
breathless attention, reading every word, instead of
merely skimming down the more sensational
columns and then turning over to see if she was
mentioned in the gossip page, which I regret to say
was her usual method.

To-day, the first paragraph which met her eye
was

AGED PEER DIES IN HARNESS

*LORD PRAGUE LIFELESS IN
UPPER HOUSE*

NIGHT WATCHMAN'S STORY

We regret to announce that Lord Prague,
G.C.B., C.V.O., etc., was found dead late last
night in the House of Lords. It is stated that his
body was discovered just before midnight by Mr.
George Wilson, the night watchman.

Mr. Wilson, when interviewed by the *Daily
Runner*, said:

'I always go into the House at least once during the night to clear up any pieces of paper, orange peel, or empty bottles that happen to have been left underneath the seats. I had been tidying for some time last night when I noticed the figure of a man half-lying on one of the benches. This did not really surprise me, as the peers often sleep on late into the night after a debate. So I went up to him and said. "Twelve o'clock, m'lord. Can I get you a cup of tea?" He took no notice and, thinking he was fast asleep, I was going to let him stay there till morning when something in his attitude made me pause and look at him more closely. I then realized that he was stone dead, so I went and fetched a policeman.'

Mr. Wilson was much shaken by his experience and says that although he has often known the peers to die in the corridors and refreshment rooms of the House he cannot recall one to have died in the House itself before.

Dr. McGregor, who was called in by the police, said that death, which was due to heart failure, had taken place some six or seven hours previously: therefore Lord Prague must have passed away in the middle of the debate on Subsidized Potatoes (which is reported on page 13).

It was stated at an early hour this morning that Lady Prague is utterly prostrated with grief.

Lord Rainford, a cousin of the late peer, said in an interview:

'I saw Prague for a moment yesterday afternoon, and he seemed in his usual good form. It has been a terrible shock to all of us, and the loss to the Nation will be irreparable.'

DASHING MORE

Absalom More, fourth Baron Prague, was born in 1838. Educated at Eton and Sandhurst, he first distinguished himself as a boy of eighteen in the Crimea, where he earned the soubriquet of Dashing More—true to his family motto, *More to the Fore*. When peace had been declared he was warmly applauded by Queen Victoria, with whom he was always a great favourite. In 1859 he succeeded to the title on the death of his father, and in 1860 he married one of the Queen's Ladies-in-Waiting, Lady Anastasia Dalloch, daughter of the Earl of Craigdalloch; who died in 1909. In 1910 he married his second wife, Florence, daughter of Mr. Leonard Jackson of Dombey Hall, Leicestershire, who survives him. Both marriages are childless, and the peerage devolves upon a distant cousin, Mr. Ivanhoe More, of Victoria Road, Kensington.

The very deepest sympathy will go out to Lady Prague, but her sorrow must needs be tempered by the thought that Dashing More died as he would have wished to die—in harness.

(Picture on the Back Page.)

Jane was entranced by this piece of news and read the paragraph over and over again. She was just about to turn to the back page for the promised picture when her eye was caught by:

THE 'BRIGHT YOUNG PEOPLE'
GO TOO FAR

MOCK FUNERAL IN LONDON NECROPOLIS

NOT FUNNY—GENERAL MURGATROYD.

It is felt that the Bright Young People have had their day and that their jokes, often in the worst possible taste, should come to an end. Yesterday afternoon a 'Mock Funeral' was held in the London Necropolis at Brookwood, where a site had been purchased in the name of Mrs. Bogus Bottom to hold the remains of Bogus Bottom, Esq. The funeral cortège, including six carriages full of weeping 'mourners,' travelled for several miles through the London streets, often causing the traffic to be delayed while it passed, and finally boarded the special Necropolis train. At Brookwood the coffin was reverently conveyed to the graveside and was just going to be lowered carefully into the grave, when the lid opened, and Mr. Julius Raynor stepped out of it, dressed as for tennis. The 'mourners' then picked up the wreaths, which were numerous and costly, and fled to waiting motor-cars.

(Pictures on the Back Page.)

HEARTLESS

The *Daily Runner*, feeling that the only way to stop these heartless pranks is by means of public opinion, sent an interviewer to the following representative men and women, who have not scrupled to express their disapproval:

Miss Martha Measles (well-known novelist):

'I have never heard that it is either clever or amusing to jest with Death...'

Sir Holden Crane (sociologist):

'If these young people would bear more children, they would hardly have the time for such foolishness...'

Bishop of Burford:

'I think it is most shameful, especially as I hear that many people doffed their hats to the cortège as it passed through London .'

Mr. Southey Roberts (satirist):

'Are these people either "Bright" or "Young"?...'

General Murgatroyd:

'It's a damned nuisance, and not funny...'

It is understood that the authorities at Brookwood are taking action, and they are very anxious to know the address of Mrs. Bogus Bottom.

Jane now turned to the back page and was rewarded by a photograph of Lord Prague in youth; and one of Julius Raynor, a ghastly figure dressed entirely in white, leaping from his coffin.

She then casually glanced at the middle page, where her attention was rooted by a photograph of Albert and a paragraph headed:

AMAZING FEAT OF YOUNG ARTIST

CRITICS ASTOUNDED BY NEW GENIUS
PICTURE FOR THE NATION?

Mr. Albert Gates (herewith) has astounded the

art critics and half social London with his exhibition of amazing pictures (now on view at the Chelsea Galleries). They are composed in many cases round real objects stuck to the canvas, such as, for instance, eyeglasses, buttons, hats, and even surgical limbs; and are of a brilliance and novelty impossible to describe, particularly No. 15, *The Absinthe Drinker*, which it is rumoured, has been bought for the Nation by Mr. Isaac Manuel. Another interesting picture is entitled: *Impression of Lady P*—and is executed entirely in bits of tweed cut into small squares. This is framed in beige mackintosh.

Mr. Gates, who left Oxford four years ago, and has since been studying art in Paris, is a tall, good-looking young man of a modest disposition. When a *Daily Runner* representative called on him after the private view of his pictures yesterday, he seemed unaware of the sensation his work had caused in art circles. 'I think it was quite a good party,' he said, referring to the private view.

Mr. Gates recently became engaged to Miss Jane Dacre, the beautiful daughter of Sir Hubert and Lady Dacre of Stow-on-the-Wold, Gloucestershire.

Jane, on reading this, became very thoughtful. She was not at all sure that she liked this sudden blaze of fame which had come so unexpectedly upon Albert. The picture which she had framed in her mind of their married life had been imagined without this new factor. She had thought of herself as being all in all to him: his one real friend, sticking to him through thick and thin, encouraging, praising and helping. Much as she admired, or thought she admired, Albert's work herself, it had never occurred to her that he might have a real success with the critics; she had imagined that such revolutionary ideas would remain unnoticed for years, except by a few of the ultra-moderns.

The telephone-bell interrupted her train of thought. She put out her hand rather absentmindedly to take off the receiver, wondering who it could be so early. Albert's voice, trembling with excitement, said:

'Have you seen the papers, darling? Yes, they're all the same. Buggins says he can't remember any exhibition to have had such notices for years and years. And I've just been talking to Isaac Manuel. He's buying *The Absinthe Drinker* for the *Tate*, my dear! and two still lifes for himself; and he's commissioned me to fresco some rooms in his new house. What d'you think of that? So it looks as if we shall have to live in London for a bit, after all. Do you mind, darling one? Of course, I said I could do nothing until our honeymoon is over, but we may have to cut it short by a week or two, I dare say. Isn't it splendid, darling? Aren't you pleased? I never for a moment thought the English critics had so much sense, did you? Where are you lunching to-day? Oh, yes, I'd forgotten. Well, meet me at the Chelsea, will you, at about one? You're not feeling ill or anything, are you? Oh, I thought you sounded rather subdued, that's all. Well, good-bye. I must go round to Manuel's now.'

As Jane hung up the receiver her eyes were full of tears.

'I couldn't feel more jealous,' she thought

miserably, 'if it were another woman. It's disgusting of me not to be pleased, but I can't help it.'

She began working herself up into a state of hysteria while she dressed. She saw all her dreams of Albert's struggle for fame, with herself helping and encouraging, of a tiny house in Paris only visited by a few loyal friends, and of final success in about ten years' time largely brought about by her own influence, falling to earth shattered.

Albert, with his looks, talents and new-found fame, would soon, she thought, become the centre of that semi-artistic social set which is so much to the fore in London. He would be courted and flattered, his opinions accepted, and his presence eagerly sought after: while she, instead of being his one real friend, the guiding star of his life, would become its rather dreary background. She imagined herself growing daily uglier and more boring. People would say: 'Yes, poor boy, he married her before he had met any other women. He must be regretting it now that it's too late.'

Jane, who at all times was inclined to take an exaggerated view of things, and whose nerves had been very much on edge since the fire in Scotland, was now incapable of thinking calmly or she would have realized that a few press notices, however favourable, and a commission from Sir Isaac Manuel, although very flattering to a young artist, do not in themselves constitute fame. She had a sort of wild vision of Albert as a pivot of public attention, already too busy being flattered and adulated to speak to her for more than a minute on the telephone. She imagined herself arriving at the Chelsea Galleries for their luncheon appointment and finding that he had forgotten all about her and gone off with some art critic and his wife instead.

At last Jane believed that all these things were quite true, and by the time she had finished dressing she was in a furious rage with Albert. Unable to contain herself, she wrote to him:

'DARLING ALBERT,

'I have been thinking about you and me, and I can see now that we should never be happy together. You have your work, and now this tremendous success has come you won't be wanting me as well, and I think it better from every point of view to break off our engagement, so good-bye, darling Albert, and please don't try to see me any more as I couldn't bear it.

'JANE.'

Quickly, for fear she should change her mind, she gave this note to the chauffeur and told him to take it round at once to Mr. Buggins' house.

She then went back to her bedroom and cried on the bed. She cried at first because her nerves were in a really bad state. After about half an hour she was crying for rage because Albert had not come round to see her or at least telephoned; but soon she was beyond tears, and her heart was broken.

'If he loved me he wouldn't let me go like that. This silence can only mean that he accepts: that the engagement is really broken off. Oh, God! how can I bear it? I can't go on living! I shall have to kill myself.'

The telephone-bell rang and Jane, with a beating heart, took off the receiver. 'This must be he!' It was her mother's sister asking what she wanted for a wedding present.

'China,' said Jane feverishly, 'china! china! china! Any sort of china! Thank you so much, Aunt Virginia.'

After this she felt that she had reached depths of despair which she did not even know to exist before. She sat in a sort of coma, and when the telephone-bell rang again, she knew that it could not be Albert.

But it was.

'Darling Jane, it's a quarter-past one. Have I got to wait here for ever?'

'Oh! is it really so late? Didn't you get my note, Albert?'

'No, what note? Can't you come, then?'

'Yes, in a moment. I wrote to say I should be late, but I won't be long now.'

'Well, hurry!'

'Yes, sweetest. Oh, I do love you!'

Jane rang up Mr Buggins.

'If there's a note from me to Albert, will you be an angel and burn it? Thank you so much. Yes, isn't it splendid! No. I've not seen him yet. We're lunching together so I must fly.'

Photoset, printed and bound in Great Britain by
REDWOOD PRESS LIMITED, Melksham, Wiltshire